A BAKER'S DOZEN
13 Chilling Indian Tales of Macabre

By

Arun 'Harry' Hariharan

Creative CROWS
PUBLISHERS LLP
the publishing & communication people

Published by

Creative CROWS
PUBLISHERS LLP
the publishing & communication people

Office: A-42, Dayanand Colony,
New Delhi(South)-110024
Mobile: +91-9953758404, +91-9833283155
Emails: ganivpanjrath@yahoo.co.in, tannaazirani@gmail.com

First Published – 2021
ISBN-13: 978-93-91526-04-7
ISBN 10: 93-91526-04-7
MRP: Rs.450/-
Book size: 5.5"x7.5"

Printed and bound by Creative Crows Publishers LLP

Preface

Horror is not a genre…it is an emotion.
-Douglas E Winter

India is an ancient land with a mystic, multi-hued and often violent past. The landscape of the country is dotted with vestiges of this tapestry. The relics of the past are not only in the form of monuments and ruins but also legends, parables and records both documented and passed down in the oral tradition.

Occult, horror and macabre have always been part of Indian folklore with tales of rabid *churails*[1], haunted *havelis*[2], *Mohini pisachas*[3], headless horsemen, possessions at *dargahs*[4] and the like, shared in hushed tones. Though normally not a very popular genre in Indian literature, horror and macabre have seen very significant contributions by authors such as Satyajit Ray (remember the chilling 'Gagan Chaudhuri's Studio'?) and Ruskin Bond (every Indian kid must have surely got goose-bumps reading 'A Face in the Dark').

I grew up on a staple of Edgar Allen Poe, Honore d'Balzac, H. P. Lovecraft, Stephen King, William Peter Blatty and the like. Thereafter, travelling to remote corners of this

[1]Female banshee
[2]Small palace or a large villa
[3]Devil in the form of a temptress
[4]Graves of Muslim holy men

vast country and visiting forgotten places that do not even figure on the map during my over two decades of service in the Indian Army, tickled the writer in me to pen down this modest collection of thirteen very 'Indian' horror tales.

All the stories are purely works of fiction though inspired in varying degrees by real incidents, people and historical events. However, each place mentioned in this book really does exist and most I have visited! Do check out the trivia section at the end of the book which gives out a little more information on some of the people, places and incidents figuring in the stories - it will help you visualise the stories better and lend realism to your read.

I surely hope you get enough goose-bumps and do look over your shoulder at least once, walking down a dark alley, after you read this book. In any case don't read this book when you are alone at night – I cannot guarantee you a good night's sleep thereafter!

-Arun 'Harry' Hariharan
Gurugram, India
October 2021

For

Janaki Hariharan, my grandmother – a self-taught woman who also was the greatest story teller I ever met!

My wife Kalpana who has been a genuine critic and an enthusiastic proof reader

And

My parents- who have always encouraged me to write from my childhood

Fear

The moon peeped out as the daylight faded
Amidst ominous clouds in dark skies
The Earth appeared tired and jaded
Engulfed by darkness full of deceit and lies

Unholy creatures lurked the countryside
Through which a lonely traveller walked
Shivering each time and quickening his stride
As he heard voices in a tongue never yet talked

A wizened claw seemed to beacon him near
And a serpent seemed to engulf his mind
For it was fear… a deep foreboding fear
In the darkness what was he to find

Uncanny silhouettes, undead creatures
Ghastly noises, eerie laughter
Seemed to be the overwhelming features
As his fear seemed to get him better

Suddenly he sat up dazed
In the safety of his cosy bed
On the wall he blankly gazed
The fears seemed conjured in his head!

Fear is the path to the Dark Side,
We believe in ghosts for they're our own creation,
It is from them we in vain hide,
…and we haunt ourselves in craven.

Foreword

Many years ago, when we were together in Foxtrot Squadron at the National Defence Academy, I'm sure neither of us could never have imagined that Arun would be writing a book one day, and that I would be writing the Foreword to it! I think the writing bug is contagious, and am glad it's bitten Arun too. I'm sure it will continue to infect him forever now.

A Baker's Dozen - 13 Chilling Indian Tales of Macabre should come with two statutory warnings - the first cautioning the readers not to read the stories just before going to sleep, lest every sound thereafter makes them jump and keeps them awake. The second warning - not to start reading it unless they have enough time at hand, since they will find it difficult to put down. Arun has put together this wonderful bouquet of tales that are fast paced, keeping the reader hanging on the edge of the seat wondering what will happen next.

The settings and locales of the stories point to Arun's keen power of observation, and the way he has knitted narratives with historical events makes the past also come alive.

I know that after finishing the book the reader will be left wanting more. So, I'm sure Arun will be getting a lot of requests for coming out with a Volume II at the earliest. I hope he's already working on that, and wishing him the very best for this and all the forthcoming volumes.

-Rohit Agarwal

Best Selling Author of books such *as Riding the Raisina Tiger (2016), Academy -Bonded for Life (2020), 1971 Indo-Pak War: Selected Stories (2020)* and *Delhi Durbar: 1911 the Complete Story (2016)*

Introduction

Who doesn't love spooky stories? Don't we all have memories of sitting around in the eerie darkness of the night, recounting stories filled with chilling suspense? Arun Hariharan's *A Baker Dozen* – a collection of thirteen well-written ghostly tales – leaves you with that creepy tingling feeling along the spine. What's lovely about this collection is that these stories are not filled with unnecessary gore or grisly violence, but follow the more classical horror route of Poe or Maupassant or our own Ruskin Bond, relying on building up suspense and then delivering the masterful twist at the end. What distinguishes the book is the depth and breadth of its span of interior India – in less than a hundred pages, Arun takes you on a tour of little-known places of the country, from the Anglo Indian colony of Mccluskieganj in Jharkhand to the dusty plains of Meerut to the bend in the South Pennar river in Tamil Nadu, packing in loads of authentic local flavour. There is considerable time travel in the book too as the short stories are set in different periods – from the Sepoy Mutiny of 1857 to the 1962 Indo-China war to more contemporary times. Arun has imaginatively used real- life incidents as the basis of many of his stories, giving them a masterful macabre twist to deliver a spine-chilling read. This is a very impressive debut.

-Chitra Narayanan
Editorial Consultant
The Hindu Business Line

Contents

Story **ONE**

SHARVARA'S HORDES

The Lord God had created all animals, and had chosen out the wolf to be his dog.
– Jacob Grimm

The huffing of the tired and frothing horse was the only sound that cut through the stillness of the night. It was way past sunset and Ronald Howard did not know exactly where he was. It had been quite a journey from Delhi, where on that fateful day of 17th May 1857, his small outpost on the banks of the River Yamuna had been overrun by the mutinous sepoys from the garrison of Meerut, some 30 miles to the East. He had been the sole survivor and had somehow managed to escape in spite of his right shoulder taking in a small amount of buck shot fire. Thankfully, the bleeding had stopped but his red tunic was stained with a dark patch of dried blood. The loss had made him weak and tired.

He had ridden into the night on his mare and had moved north along the Western banks of the Yamuna hoping to reach Sonipat which still had a garrison loyal to the East India Company.

The horse slowed down to a trot and finally to a walk. He pulled out his pocket watch (which surprisingly was with him and still ticking) and squinted in the moonlight to see the time. It was still one hour to midnight. He as well as the horse were tired and thirsty.

"Need to find some water fast!" he thought wryly, his lips parched and dry in the sweltering heat of an Indian summer night. Though the scorching heat of the sun was not there, the air was hot and dry, sucking out the moisture from the man and the beast he rode.

The mutineers had pursued him until it was dark after which they noisily headed back. But in the bargain, he had to leave the river bank to shake them off; and as a result, did not know how far he had steered off his course. All he could now hope for was to wait until sunrise and then discreetly find his way to friendly territories.

The moon was thankfully up and the surroundings were somewhat visible in the shimmering moonlight. An arid scrub jungle covered the entire area towards his right and a low hill range flanked his left. He crossed a couple of rivulet beds, but they were parched and without any sign of water.

The exhausted horse finally gave up and sat down on its haunches.

Howard cursed under his breath and muttered, "If the rebels don't get me – thirst surely will."

He dismounted and looked around for some sign of life… and water. He suddenly stopped at his tracks – did he hear a movement near the hill to his left? Indeed, there was a rustling sound coming from some 300 yards away – the kind of sound made by a small animal moving through dry undergrowth. Not wanting to take any chances now that he was injured and unarmed, Howard quickly hid himself behind a boulder and observed. After all, the areas around Delhi still teemed with rebels and the ruthless thugs – a criminal sect of robbers infamous for garrotting their victims with finesse.

The disturbance was caused by what appeared to be a small dog or a jackal. He realized it was dog when it came close to the horse, which was still on its haunches, and barked nervously.

"If there is a dog here, there must be some habitation nearby," thought Howard.

Howard then saw a yellowish light flicker half-way up the hill and decided to explore. He walked through the thicket and moved towards the light, trying to make as little sound as possible, through the thorny *kikar*[5] trees. As he drew closer he could make out the shape of what appeared to be a small Hindu temple. He neared the clearing and cautiously looked around. It was a temple with a conical spire and an oil lamp flickered tentatively in the breeze outside the shrine.

"Let me not alarm anybody here…but I'm sure I'll be able to at least get some food and water," he thought as he tip-toed into the clearing looking around carefully.

He couldn't help glancing inside the shrine. He had been in India for a quite few years now, and could understand and speak Hindustani quite well, being from a Native Infantry Regiment. Though Hinduism was complicated as far as Gods were concerned (there were just too many of them) – he could recognize the common ones: Siva, Rama, Krishna and the like. But the idol in this temple was a surely out of the ordinary. It was a fearsome looking God with a Dog's snarling visage. He shrugged his shoulders and continued to search for a source of water.

[5] Indian Gum Arabic tree

He finally found what he wanted – a leather bladder full of water hanging on a small tree towards the right of the temple. He picked up the bladder and thirstily drank the cool water. It tasted a little metallic but appeared to be clean.

Suddenly he heard a cacophonic sound of his horse neighing loudly and a number of dogs barking simultaneously. The sound came from the direction of the spot where he had left the horse. His thirst quenched, he hung the bladder with the remaining water around his shoulder and instinctively picked up an iron scimitar embedded in the soil outside the shrine and headed towards the sound. He was surely not getting a good feeling.

The moon hid behind a cloud as he was coming down the spur. His feet skidded in the loose gravel and he slid down the slope pretty rapidly. He was sweating profusely. Howard's shoulder was now starting to hurt. "Must be all the exertion…" he thought.

As he reached closer to the place where he had left the tired horse, he stopped in his tracks struck by horror and hid himself behind an outcrop on the hill-side. He could see a pack of what appeared to be 20 odd dogs (or were they wolves?) mauling the horse as the unfortunate animal ineffectually tried to fight them off. Wounded, and unarmed barring the rusty scimitar, Howard could only watch the one-sided match of death as the dogs tore the poor mare down after a few minutes. Howard had this sudden urge to turn around and run, but froze at the spot, realizing that he was too close to the dogs and any movement on his part could attract attention towards himself.

There was then an eerie baying sound from a distance. Howard squinted to discern the source of the sound. From the darkness of the thicket, onto the moonlit clearing appeared a huge black animal. He had seen quite a few wolves in India, but this one was surely a freak. It was really big – almost the size of a small horse. He rubbed his eyes in disbelief but the spectre was still there. The other dogs moved aside as the wolf leapt at the stricken horse with a blood curdling growl. Howard winced as he saw the beast grab the neck of the horse and bite off its head, finally ending the poor animal's misery. He then heard a low whistling sound. Among the same shadows where the wolf had come from, he could now see a human form emerge. Though he could not clearly make out the features, he saw a smallish man wearing rustic Indian clothes with a wooden staff in his hand and a big turban on his head. He was surprised to see the fierce big wolf meekly go and rub itself against him. The man in turn petted the animal. He yelled some unintelligible command and all the other dogs pounced on the horse's body and started devouring it noisily.

The man to went up to the carcass of the horse and ripped out a chunk of meat with his bare hands and then devoured it – more like an animal rather than a human. The whole drama was uncanny and nauseating. The air was still and stuffy. Howard had this sudden urge to vomit, but controlled himself.

A cool breeze had begun blowing from the direction of the hill towards the clearing. It somewhat relieved his badly frayed nerves. Suddenly, the wolf seemed to be getting a little uneasy as it began growling with its snout up in the air. The man also looked up from his grisly meal. To his horror – the man and the wolf were now looking up towards his direction!

"Oh my God…! The wind must have carried my scent," he thought, as panic gripped him.

The man, the wolf and the other dogs now had started moving in his direction. Howard got up and started scrambling up the hill. The barking of the dogs was getting louder. The pack was moving fast led by the big wolf. The man still stood in the clearing, not moving.

The blood loss had made Howard weak and he was completely spent as he broke into a run. But the dogs were gaining fast. The first few of the pack caught up with him baring their fangs furiously and trying to go for his legs. The dogs were feral with scrawny and with dirty coats. He slashed with the scimitar and killed the first dog and injured a second, but the third got his ankle and he tripped over. To his horror, a huge shadow loomed as the wolf pounced on him and locked its huge jaws on his right thigh spurting out blood as he yelled in pain. The big animal now dragged him down the slope as he ineffectually tried to fight it away. Two of the other dogs too pulled at his left leg as they too began dragging him down. The scimitar had fallen from his hand as he helplessly allowed himself to be pulled by the animals.

At the base of the hill the dogs stopped as the man whistled at them. In the moonlight, Howard could see the man looking down at him. He had an ugly swarthy face and grinned through blood stained teeth at Howard.

"Who are you?" asked Howard in a hoarse voice in his best Hindustani.

"Sharvara!" said the man before the big wolf closed its huge jaws around Howard's neck.

Epilogue

Captain Anderson with a small posse of the 15th Cavalry and some native *sowars*[6] under *Jemadar*[7] Behram Khan had ridden out from Umballa[8] early in the morning. It was almost three months since the unfortunate happenings of the mutiny. Delhi had since been taken back by General Nicholson.

Though the scrounge of *thuggee*[9] had been effectively eliminated by Colonel Sleeman[10] more than a decade ago, in the 1840s, there still had been frequent incidents of lawlessness and violent crime in the areas adjacent to the

[6]Native Indian cavalryman

[7] Native Indian Officer

[8]Modern day Ambala, Haryana

[9]Acts of the Thugs, who were organised gangs of professional robbers and murderers. Refer trivia section for more details

[10] Later Major-General Sir William Henry Sleeman KCB

Yamuna, largely uncharted by the British. The small force under Anderson had ridden out in pursuit of a particularly nasty band of *gurjars*[11] who were tormenting British convoys on the Western banks of the Yamuna.

The troop had ridden long and hard and had left the main road connecting Delhi to the Punjab about 2 hours ago. They were now crossing an arid scrub covered area with a low hill range flanking their left; not many had traversed this region since the map did not give out much. Anderson motioned the group to slow down as he saw clearing a little further ahead. He signalled Behram to go ahead and check out the area with another *sowar*. Behram moved ahead and came back in sometime.

"*Sahib*! Hurry up you must see this!" he said urgently.

Anderson moved ahead and saw the skeletal remains of a horse with its saddle intact lying next to the track. Behram nervously pointed out a little further ahead. A tattered red uniform wrapped the headless skeleton with no signs of flesh on it. To his horror Anderson realized that it was what remained of the body of a British soldier.

"Lieutenant… Ronald Howard," he read out after seeing the badges of rank on the uniform and the name tab which was still pinned on. "Poor bugger escaped the rebels but something got him here and the vultures have picked him clean."

A brass pocket watch was still chained to the pocket of the tunic. Anderson picked it up and pocketed it.

"Must find out his Regiment and send this across to them…" he thought.

The party sombrely dug a grave and Anderson buried Howard's remains and placed and makeshift cross over it.

[11] A nomadic tribe

The sun was right overhead and it reflected off a fairly large stone structure halfway up the hill amidst the thick *kikar* under growth.

"Any idea…what that is Behram?" asked Anderson.

Behram just shrugged.

Taking Behram and two more *sowars* with him, Anderson made a small trek to the structure. It appeared to be some kind of a temple and was in ruins with undergrowth almost completely overwhelming the structures. A rotting water bladder still hung on the small tree. The main structure had the statue of a weird looking dog-faced God at its centre.

Behram suddenly said, "*Sahib*! I think that is the old Sharvara temple…temple of the dog faced God who guards the gates of the nether-world[12]. Had heard about it from my Uncle who happened to ride with Sleeman *sahib*. From his description it should indeed be around here somewhere. Thug Peelu one of the most notorious thugs, lived here many years back. Unlike other thugs, he never used to garrotte his victims. They say he had a pack of feral dogs and a big wolf which was supposed to have had the spirit of the devil in it. The pack used to drag down his victims and devour them after he had robbed them. He was finally caught and hanged by Colonel Sleeman *sahib* during his anti thuggee campaign around 1840. All his dogs too were culled. Except they say that the wolf was never found!"

[12] Refer trivia section for more details

Story **TWO**

KARUPPU RAYAN'S RETRIBUTION

Words have no power to impress the mind without the exquisite horror of their reality.
-Edgar Allan Poe

It had been an easier job than I imagined. No violence, no alarms, no nothing. The fierce *Karuppu Rayan*[13] , the ancient village guardian deity, seemed to be ironically kind to me. The *Karuppu Rayan* temple was almost pre-historic; and was located in the middle of the Gudalur Forest. It was accessible only through a small

[13]Literally- 'Black Guardian'. Refer trivia section for more details.

foot track through the rainforest. The God or *Rayan's* fierce faced idol must have been a few thousand years old and worn with offerings of *ghee*[14] and numerous *abhishekas*[15] through the ages. The equally ancient banyan tree almost covered the little shrine with its gnarled branches. Towards the end of the clearing was an altar which had a flat rock in the centre and an iron trident which normally had one lemon each impaled on its each spike. The altar was used for animal sacrifices (and some say for human sacrifice until as late as the 1950s). The rock was dark and stained by the blood of the numerous animals (and humans) decapitated there.

No one dared to venture to the temple after dusk due to the presence of a large number of tigers, leopards and wild elephants in the forest – and as legend had it, for some other unknown sinister reasons also. It was said that anyone who dared to disturb the *Rayan* in his slumber after dusk and trod on his holy ground was never seen or heard of again. It was also said that he was the patron deity of thieves and forest brigands, who apparently had spread the story, so that they could safely take refuge and review their booty away from unwanted eyes. Whatever the theory, people did not want to take a chance and generally avoided the place after dark.

The annual fair of the temple was always held in the second week of November, and this year it was no different. The annual fair had just got over a day ago and the space was littered with garbage, a remnant of human presence.

The Rayan's ornaments were priceless and were held safely for generations with the *Zamindar*[16] of Gudalur except for 14 days of the year; 12 days of the fair and 2 days hence up to the next full moon when the final sacrifice was done and the accoutrements of Rayan's idol in the temple, were returned to the safety of the *Zamindar's* armoury. It was

[14]Clarified butter

[15]Liquid offerings poured over the idol

[16]Feudal landlord

generally unguarded during the night barring a padlock put on the temple door, for the simple reason that for centuries, no one dared to think of disturbing the *Rayan* during the night, let alone touch either the idol or the jewels.

It was this fear of the demon-God in people and their faith that he could take care of himself that made my job so easy. Of course, I too must confess that the very aura of the place at night played on my nerves; but two swigs of fresh toddy cleared my mind of unnecessary fears and added steel to my tingling nerves.

The ambient light was bright, it being a day before the full moon. A blow of the crowbar brought down the old padlock and I could clearly see *Rayan's* gold and silver ornaments decked in diamonds and rubies of ancient origin, glistening as though they had a life of their own, as a beam of silvery moon light fell upon them. I quickly removed all the accoutrements and stuffed them into the gunny sack I was carrying. However, the fearsome primordial form of *Rayan* with big protruding eyes, fangs jutting out at the edges of his mouth and a garland of human skulls did give me the creeps and I wanted to leave the sanctum sanctorum as early as I could. All I could think of the blissful life I could lead with Lakshmi, the girl I loved, after disposing of my priceless booty.

I quickly checked the chamber to make sure nothing of value had been left behind and hefting my sack, which was rather heavy by now, I went out of the small temple. I was actually sweating profusely and was relieved when a cool waft of breeze blew and cooled not only my warm body but also my frayed nerves.

Suddenly there was a commotion in the thicket to my left and a number of birds went flying out of the trees as though disturbed. I realized that they were actually not birds but bats which had been disturbed from their perches high up on the trees and the rocky outcrop towards the North of the clearing. I quickly hid myself behind some bushes and observed the whole scene for more than half an hour to make sure that no one was around.

The bats finally settled down and so did my throbbing veins. I hefted the gunny sack and after actually apologizing to *Rayan* under my breath (I don't know why I did that) I moved down the track into the darkness of the forest onwards to a life of riches, love and freedom.

I knew the forest like the back of my hand and did not need any map or lights to negotiate it. The ambient light was good enough for me to find my way about. I should be at the river bank in an hour I thought to myself. I had placed a small row boat at the river which would take me down stream, across and far, far away by the time people realized what had happened.

I was nearing the river bank as I could hear the frogs croaking and smell the dankness of rotting vegetation. There was also a distinct putrid smell in the area, which seemed somewhat familiar. It was the smell of bat droppings; a distinct smell normally associated with caves and dark spaces. Apparently quite a few bats inhabited the crevices in the ancient trees which lined the river bank.

Yet again, it was either me or a monkey or something else that disturbed the bats and they started squeaking and flapping around the trees. Suddenly, the din of their squeaking grew louder and the sound of flapping wings rose to almost a crescendo. I immediately took cover behind a large tree not wanting to take any chances, and decided to move once the disturbed bats had settled down and the cause of their disturbance had also left.

I must have dozed off for a few minutes, but awoke with a start as something whirled past my ear and lightly brushed my face. I tried to focus in the darkness where a little moonlight was shimmering in for me to be able to just about discern the shapes of the trees and bushes. The trees were all dark forms against a dim silvery background.

Were my eyes playing tricks on me? I swore I could see one of the looming shadowy forms of the trees move albeit very slowly. I determined not to let panic settle in at this stage and held on to my ground and tried to focus into the darkness once again. But the dark form was indeed moving and seemed to be coming closer. The form was huge and now I could hear a distinct whirling and flapping sound as though a number of wings were flapping simultaneously.

I decided that I had had enough of bravado and decided to make a run towards the river bank with was less than 200 yards away. I did not like the look of what was happening. I ran with the gunny sack on my back. The golden bowl and a few other utensils that I had picked up from the temple made a light clanging sound as I ran as fast as I could towards the river. The whirling sound also increased. Suddenly my toe struck the gnarled root of one of the ancient trees and before I realized, I lay sprawled on the ground. Luckily, there didn't seem to be any major injury and hence, I tried getting up rubbing my bruised knees and elbows and felt around for the gunny sack which had fallen on the grass nearby. As I went to pick up the sack, the whirling sound which seemed very close now, suddenly changed to the sound of a thousand bats squeaking together; and as I looked up, it was a huge black form roughly of human shape but composed of hundreds of bats as though they were tied together by some invisible force. The form then engulfed me.

The sunlight seemed to hurt my eyes. Where the hell am I? I wondered. I opened my eyes to realize that day had dawned and I was near the temple once again. There were two people talking near the temple, one of whom I recognized as the head priest.

"Someone tried to rob the temple last night…see the lock is broken," said the priest to the man pointing towards the broken lock.

"Is anything missing?" asked the man.

"Surprisingly no…I have rechecked three times. We seem to live in bad times – this kind of thing happens almost every year now, but never has anything ever been found missing from the temple. I trust *Karuppu Rayan* is quite capable of protecting himself!" replied the priest smiling and added, "I will get the locks changed immediately."

"By the way this place smells quite a bit," said the man.

"It is the bat droppings. Their numbers seem to be increasing every year," said the priest. "You are right. They say that they are blessed by Rayan the Lord of the forest and in turn, they protect him," said the man.

I suddenly realized that all the while, I was actually looking down upon the two men and seeing everything upside down. The sunlight had started hurting my eyes badly and I needed a dark crevice to rest now.

Story **THREE**

THE GAISAL CLUB

We make up horrors to help us cope with the real ones.
-Stephen King

He realized he shouldn't have had that plate of *biriyani*[17] at New Jalpaiguri Railway Station. It was playing tricks on his stomach. His body clock was in a mess anyway, after staying awake at nights for the last 3 months. The restive province of Assam had gone through an election in the summer of 2006 and Karan, Captain Karan Sharma of the Garhwal Rifles had played a small part in ensuring that it had gone off peacefully without too much of mischief from insurgents. His last six

[17]Spicy rice cooked with meat

months in North Lakhimpur with his battalion on 'election' duty had been taxing with intense patrolling at nights taking a toll on his health. Anyway, he was looking forward to his well-earned 2 months leave and spending quality time in Delhi with mom and dad as well as Sheela. He had made up his mind to propose to Sheela this time.

He had booked himself on the flight from Dibrugarh to Delhi but the evil August weather had rendered the flight service erratic and he was actually thankful to land up with a Two-Tier AC seat in the Brahmaputra Mail at such a short notice. It was not the fastest of trains, but he was happy that he could be on his way to Delhi without wasting any time.

Karan tried to ignore the happenings in his stomach and plugged on his iPod and played his favourite Eagles belting out 'Tulsa Time' and tried to get forty winks. His body clock was just refusing to collaborate. Karan had two swigs from his hip flask and felt the raw Old Monk Rum burning its way through his gullet into his stomach. It was past 11 p.m., and the other passengers were fast asleep. He could hear a cacophony of snores and heard the fat guy next to him turn and fart, all in his sleep. He was actually envious of how anyone could sleep with such abandon. Slowly, Karan too drifted into a fitful slumber.

Karan got up with a start; his stomach was cramping badly and he had to use the toilet. He moved out of the AC compartment towards the toilet. The train was stationary. He peeped out of the window on his way to the toilet. The train was halted at a way side station. He squinted to see the name of the station. The board illuminated by the yellow light of a lone halogen spelt out 'Gaisal' in English and Hindi and Bangla. Karan went to the toilet and tried to get some relief. But the ailment seemed more in the mind rather in the bowels. "I think some fresh air will do me good!" he thought wryly finding no relief in the toilet.

Loosening the latch of the door he stepped outside on

the platform. His watch showed the time as 1:20 a.m. It was late and there was not a single soul at the station. The air smelt of petrichor and the sound of crickets in concert was a welcome relief from the more obnoxious decibels emanating in his coach.

"I wonder why the train is standing here?" thought Karan. "Must be to provide crossing for some other train," he decided.

'Gaisal'. The name seemed vaguely familiar. "I wonder where I heard this name earlier," thought Karan. Deciding that he must get back to bed, Karan turned around, when he heard the hoot of a distant train approaching the station. The 'rat a tat' of the train's wheels rolling on the tracks was rhythmic.

"I guess we should be on our way once this bugger passes," he muttered under his breath and headed back to his coach.

Suddenly, he heard a sickening sound – the sound of metal clashing against metal and thereafter an explosion! Something had gone drastically wrong. He found the bogies of Brahmaputra Mail crumple one after the other in front of him like a pack of cards. The engine of the oncoming train had ploughed into the static Brahmaputra Mail at great speed. His coach went up in a ball of fire and was thrown at least 20 feet in the air due to the collision. The co-passengers were tossed out like a bunch of skittles, burning and screaming.

Suddenly he felt someone clutching his feet. He was horrified to find a young fellow with a wisp of beard, both his legs severed and bleeding profusely, tugging at his pants and murmuring, "Help me! Help me please…"

Karan wanted to scream, but the sound just choked in his throat. Clutching his throat, he tried to shout and call for help. He was sweating profusely, wondering what he should do next.

A sudden jolt woke him from his terror-stricken stupor.

He sat up in abject horror. There was silence all around and suddenly it was all very quiet, barring the snoring of co-passengers. Karan sat up with a jerk, banging his head against the roof of the coach! He was utterly disoriented. Suddenly he realized that it all had been a bad nightmare! He was still very much in the train.

"It must have been the rum and that stupid *biriyani* that I ate," he decided. But he was wide awake now and looked at the luminous dials of his watch. It said 1:22.

The train jerked to a halt. He decided to take a walk and get over his disturbing nightmare. He plugged on his iPod back into his ears and selected his favourite 'Hotel California'. He jumped down from his upper berth and found all others in his coach fast asleep. The train was now static, probably an unscheduled halt. He peeped out of the window and saw the yellow board of a station dimly lit by a single incandescent bulb. He could not read the name but decided to get down and have a smoke to calm down his jarred nerves and disturbed stomach.

Hoisting himself out of the coach onto the platform which looked vaguely familiar, Karan lit a cigarette and took a deep drag. He almost jumped out of his skin when someone tapped his shoulder from behind.

"What the…?" he almost shouted utterly startled.

He turned around to find an old man with a lantern in his hand and in a railway uniform. In the dim light he saw the glint of a name tab on his lapel which said 'CP Dey, ASM[18]'. In deeply Bengali accented English, the railway man profusely apologized for startling him.

"Sorry Sir! I didn't mean to scare you. I am the Assistant Station Master here. Saw you down here. It's been a long night for me; just wanted to borrow a smoke."

"Of course!" said Karan extending his pack of Gold

---

[18]Assistant Station Master

Flake to the ASM.

He gladly picked up a cigarette and lit up from Karan's lighter.

"Dey *Sahib*[19], what happened? Will we be held up long?"

"Sir, there has been a derailment near Kishanganj and it might take 3-4 hours before your train gets clearance to move."

"Oh God! Why do all these things happen only to me?" thought Karan wryly.

The orchestra of crickets and frogs was creating a racket and fire-flies were darting in the darkness of the moonless night. The mosquitoes started buzzing and biting his arms and face.

"Can I offer you a cup of tea, Sir?" said Dey. "We can go over to the railwaymen's club very near here," he said pointing to a light at a distance.

Sensing that Karan seemed wary, Dey smiled and continued, "Don't worry Sir! Neither the train nor you can leave unless I give clearance. So, you will not miss your train!"

They walked down a small rutted path towards the light. It just struck Karan that the station was pitch dark. Even the lone incandescent bulb seemed off now.

As they neared the club building, Karan read the old-fashioned board put up on the building in the dim light '*Gaisal Railwaymen's Club*'. "Gaisal!" he wondered a little startled – the same station he had seen in his dream. It also just struck him that he had never asked Dey the name of the station until now.

He heard some banter coming from inside the building.

"Is there someone in the club?" he asked Dey.

"Oh! Just a few friends who stay there. You will meet all

[19]Honorific title

of them."

The 'club house' was a ramshackle 2 room affair, built in a different era and not maintained too much since then. Two 60 W bulbs hung from the ceiling and a motley group of three more people were seated on old fashioned spring sofas with faded upholstery. Karan was not feeling too comfortable. The name of the station too was disturbing him. Where had he heard it before and why had the name figured in his dream?

"Please join us Captain *Sahib*," said one of the figures in Hindi.

He could not clearly see the figure's face as he sat in one corner of the room. Karan froze. How does he know that I am a Captain? I have not even introduced myself to Dey until now. The voice too seemed familiar.

"How do you know that I am a Captain?" blurted Karan.

"Relax! We always do a background check before giving membership to the Gaisal Club to anyone," said the figure.

"Membership? What the hell is he talking Dey *Sahib*?" said Karan turning to Dey, with irritation in his voice.

"Don't worry! He is one of our original founding members. He's just trying to be friendly. Please sit. I have already ordered tea." replied Dey.

"I am not comfortable here – I want to go back to the train. Thank you but I don't feel like having tea anymore," said Karan turning towards the door and instinctively plugging in the earphones of his iPod and switching it on.

The Eagles were still playing Hotel California from the last place where he switched it off -

'Last thing I remember, I was
Running for the door
I had to find the passage back
To the place I was before
"Relax," said the night man,
"We are programmed to receive.
You can check-out any time you like,

But you can never leave!'"

A chill ran down his spine – the words seemed to somewhat uncannily suit his current predicament. He started to run now up to the door. The thin figure at the corner now had moved up to the door. Karan's heart froze when he saw the face of the figure in the light – he was the same young man with amputated legs who had tugged at his feet asking for help in his dream.

"Wha…what is this? And who are you?"

"Don't worry Sir. I believe we met just some time back. I am Yash Khurana formerly student of IIM Calcutta and now a permanent member of the Gaisal Club. I am sorry I cannot let you go! One of the cardinal rules of the Club is that once your membership is accepted – you cannot leave!"

Karan was both angry and scared now. He pushed aside the figure opened the door and rushed towards the station. Running hard and sweating profusely he reached the station. The lights were back. To his horror he found that there was no train in the station.

Holding his head with both hands in despair, he thought, "I cannot definitely go back to those psychos again. There is something definitely wrong with them."

He saw a light glow in the ASM's office and ran there.

"Perhaps I can find a schedule for the next train to get out of this wretched place," he murmured to himself.

The office was bare except for an old table, chair, some battered sofas and an old-fashioned magneto phone on the table. The roof was full of sooty cobwebs. A calendar hung on the wall with its cover sheet showing August 1999. An old clock hung on the wall with its needles struck at 1:22.

"Strange – this was the time I got off the train!" he wondered recalling checking out his watch when he had got up from sleep. "These guys have not even bothered to change the calendar since 1999…weird indeed!"

An old board listed the schedules of all trains passing through the station. It was located at the far end of the room. As he got closer to read the board, he tripped on a peg table. The table toppled, spilling the lone newspaper it held. He instinctively picked up the newspaper. It was a yellowed edition of the *Times of India* dated 3rd August 1999. The headline sent a chill down his spine. It read "India's Worst Rail Disaster Ever Claims 290 Lives at Gaisal in West Bengal"[20]. The report went on to state that at around 1:22 a.m. in the morning of 2nd August 1999, the Brahmaputra Mail and Awadh Assam Express had a massive collision at Gaisal Station killing nearly 300 people and injuring over 500. It had emerged after early investigations that, it had been caused due to negligence of the ASM of Gaisal, CP Dey. Distraught over the accident, the ASM had committed suicide on the same day by hanging himself in his office. He gingerly scanned through the inner pages of the paper which had some graphic images of the accident. One of the pictures caught his attention – it was that of a young man whose legs had been crushed in the accident. The picture had a small write-up below it:

"Yash Khurana, first year student of IIM Calcutta was going to Delhi on vacation. He was badly injured and later succumbed to his injuries at the Railwaymen's Club which was being used as a makeshift hospital for treating the seriously wounded cases."

He heard footfalls behind him. He veered around to find Yash and Dey standing there grinning ear to ear.

"Time to go back to the Club Captain *Sahib* – you are ours now!" said Dey.

---

[20]Refer trivia section for more details

Yash added "Didn't I tell you earlier…? You can check-out any time you like, but you can never leave!"

Write-up in the *Times of India*, Kolkata edition 3rd August 2006:

"An Army officer identified as Captain Karan Sharma was found dead with his head decapitated on the tracks at Gaisal Railway Station on the New Jalpaiguri - Kishanganj Sector. Police have stated that prima facie it appears to be a case of accidental death wherein the officer probably hung out of the moving train, lost his balance and was run over by the oncoming Awadh Assam Express. Time of death - between 1:20 a.m. and 1:30 a.m."

Story **FOUR**

SÉANCE AT PATHARUGHAT

A ghost that would voluntarily hang about a Dak Bungalow would be mad of course; but so many men have died mad in Dak Bungalows that there must be a fair percentage of lunatic ghosts.

- Rudyard Kipling

It happened during my initial years in the Police service, in the early 1990s when I was posted as the Sub Divisional Police Officer in Upper Assam. It was raining cats and dogs (as it does most of the time in those parts) and the sun was already setting though it was just 4:00 p.m. Having nothing to do, now that there was a lull in crime and insurgency owing to the heavy monsoons which rendered any commuting in almost the whole of Assam unviable barring in risky country boats across swollen rivers and streams, I was looking forward to the evening invite for drinks and dinner at Chatterjee's house.

Chatterjee was a Tea Planter who owned the sprawling Patharughat Tea Estate on the banks of the mighty Brahmaputra. He lived with his congenial wife Suchitra in the century old Estate House. Tea business was undergoing a recession for quite a few years now and Chatterjee was postponing the annual change of tea bushes for the last two years now. The auction houses at Calcutta had not been kind and the base price of the auction was steadily going down for the last three years, affecting the very viability of the business.

But Chatterjee was a *khandani raees*; or rich by inheritance and the rental from the houses, warehouses and shops owned by the family in Calcutta and Agartala more than took care of any deficit. In any case Chatterjee and his wife had known no life beyond the tea estate for the last 30 years and could not think of moving on to a big city or a fast-paced routine of the city. They preferred the crumbling colonial splendour of their bungalow and the family like relations they had with the employees of the estate, many of them third generation at Patharughat, quite like Chatterjee himself. His grandfather had bought the estate from its erstwhile British owners in 1947, who themselves had established it during the early 1900s.

In the two years I had been learning the ropes as a young Indian Police Service (IPS) officer in the Patharughat-Darrang area, the Chatterjees had actually become very good friends – more so because they were the only people who somewhat gelled to my westernized sensibilities and with whom I could converse freely in English.

Today was a special invite as they had some guests over and Suchitra had got a special Bengali meal prepared – *machher-jol*[21] et al. She knew my weakness for good food and I had to

[21]A kind of fish curry

be part of the invite list, (not that it ran very long)!

A 15-minute Jeep ride through the driving rain saw me reach the estate house. As always, Chatterjee was at the porch to welcome me, along with Dipankar their old servant.

"DSP *sahib* good to see you. Do come in!" said Chatterjee enthusiastically as we moved into the Bungalow.

Suchitra looked radiant in spite of her advanced years dressed in a traditional Bengali sari.

"Hi Ajay! So nice to see you. On time as always...a policeman to the core!" she said shaking hands with me. "Meet Noyontika, my niece...she studies something at Jadavpur University," said Suchitra waving towards a 20-something girl and then towards a boy with a scraggly beard of around the same age, "...and Debashish, her friend from college."

I shook hands with both as Suchitra introduced me. "This is Mr. Ajay Singh, Deputy Superintendent of Police... he is our nearest neighbour and a dear friend," she added with a wink.

Both Noyontika and her friend appeared to be Leftist types with a carefully unkempt look and 'could not care less' look in their eyes. Noyontika had definitely inherited her aunt's stunning good looks and beautiful dark eyes. She started the conversation first.

"Mr. Singh, it is really a pleasure to meet you. Honestly you are the first flesh and blood police officer I have actually met in my life.".

"Ma'am the pleasure is entirely mine! By the way, make it Ajay!" I said.

It was actually after a long time that I was in the company of a young lady, a beautiful one at that!

"Then you better make it Noyon and Debu!" added the boy.

The evening passed on with banter and quite a few drinks form the Chatterjees' well stocked bar. I was feeling heady with the drink and also the company of Noyon who was sitting next to me when Suchitra announced, "Hope no one is really hungry, dinner will take some more time. I suggest we pick up one more drink each!"

Suddenly, Noyon hit upon a bright idea. "The night is dark and it is raining cats and dogs and we are in the middle of nowhere. Time to try some occult!"

I was more than keen to try whatever the pretty young thing did but Suchitra intervened.

"What are you talking Noyon? Are you nuts?"

"Don't worry Aunt Suchi we have a brave soldier to protect us," said Noyon winking at me.

"Do you guys know anything about planchets?" asked Noyon.

"Are you mad Noyon?" protested Suchitra again.

"Relax Auntie! It is all bull shit. None of this works. Let her have her fun... she picked up this damned Ouija board in Calcutta and has been wanting to try it out sometime; and right now, she's drunk!" said Debu in a bored tone.

"Suchi! I think Debu is right. All this is superstition," added Chatterjee.

"Okay...okay! do what you like. But don't blame me if something goes wrong!" said an exasperated Suchitra.

"Cool Auntie! I did some studying on the subject. All we require is this Ouija board which basically has alphabets, some drawings and also words like 'Yes' and 'No' printed at diagonal ends and of course, a medium..." said Noyon.

The old bungalow was built on an area of about four acres amidst the tea estate. About one part of this was devoted to a small pond which was used to raise fish; and some area was earmarked for avocado and guava plantations. On one end of the compound was an old banyan tree which had a small structure underneath it. From where we were sitting the structure was visible through the French windows as it was lit by a lone 40-watt incandescent bulb hanging on the perimeter fence.

"Hello! What is that Auntie?" asked Noyon pointing to the lime washed platform like structure that shone in the yellow light of the bulb.

"Oh that…that is an old grave of some *gora sahib*[22] who lived here long ago… No one knows whose it is. It has been here ever since and people say that it was here even before the estate came up. In fact, this house is older than the estate and I believe was the erstwhile Government Dak Bungalow[23], before the British founders of the estate purchased it and converted it into the estate house…but why do you ask?" said Suchitra.

There was an evil glint in Noyon's eyes as she replied with a mischievous smile. "I think we have got our spirit for the night…we will wake up this old *sahib* from his slumber."

"Are you mad!" said Suchitra almost shouting. "I don't believe much in this calling of spirits stuff…but this is taking it too far! You don't know what consequences it can lead to."

I too got a little worried now. Though a rationalist myself, experiences in the Police had taught me to respect certain things which were beyond human comprehension – and this seemed to be one.

"Noyon… I don't think that meddling with the *sahib's* spirit would be such a good idea" I said.

"Now don't tell me our brave policeman is scared!" retorted Noyon mockingly and continued, "Oh come on guys, nothing bad will happen, trust me! See the rain has stopped completely and the stars are out. It will be real fun doing this on a dramatic backdrop."

To cut the long story short – Noyon finally had her way and we all moved out across the lawn to the small structure. The structure itself was a small platform, about 10 feet x 8 feet, with the grave in the centre. The grave was typical of

[22]European Officer

[23]Rest House. Refer trivia section for more details on Dak Bungalows.

late 19th – early 20th century pattern with an unpolished granite slab and a sandstone head stone. The headstone and grave were covered with moss. Noyon shone a torch at the headstone and scraped the moss. Surprisingly it had no name or any other marking on it. Noyon excitedly placed the Ouija board on the lime washed grave and placed a small piece of cork as the concentration block.

Noyon decided to be the scribe or the recorder for the séance. We placed pillows on the sheet near the grave for comfort and the four of us (Suchitra decided to drop out as she was still supervising the cooking) sat around it with our index fingers on the cork block. Debu had started to meditate, invoking the spirit of the *sahib*.

At about ten minutes to 9 p.m., there was a rapid movement on the planchet. We could barely keep our fingers on the cork.

"I have come," said Noyon in an excited voice. We realized she had followed the cork.

"Would you like to reveal yourself?" asked Debu.

"Yes" spelled the cork.

"Who are you?" continued Debu.

"B-a-r-r-i-n-g-t-o-n" spelled the cork.

I was feeling queasy now. Honestly, I had never ever experienced anything like this. We heard a flutter of wings. We realized that a number of bats were now gathering on the old tree above us and also hanging on the electric cable.

Noyon, Debu and Chatterjee appeared equally shocked and we looked at each other in the dim light.

"Noyon…this has to stop," whispered Chatterjee hoarsely.

"Wait Uncle! The excitement has just begun…just a few minutes more," Noyon begged.

"How did you die?" asked Debu.

The reply did not quite make any sense.

"I did not die. I was cursed by the *igu*."

Noyon was rapidly recording all this on a piece of paper.

I had this sudden urge to relieve myself and also re-fill my whiskey. I would be dishonest if I were to say that I was not scared of what I had just seen - it was very unnerving. Leaving the three at the location I walked back into the house and went to the wash room. After relieving myself I came to the living room and refilled my glass.

"How much time are you all going to take…? Dinner is almost done," said Suchitra smiling at me.

"What's wrong Ajay? Why are you looking pale?" she asked seeing my disturbed face.

"What's an *igu*?" I suddenly asked her.

"An *igu*…well let me think, seem to have heard it somewhere," said Suchitra. "Let me ask Gohain *da*[24] ," she continued going towards the kitchen.

Gohain *da* was their wizened old cook, almost 80 years of age, whose family had served the Chatterjees and before them the English owners of the Estate.

"Ajay! Ajay! come here!" I heard Suchitra frantically call me to the kitchen in a few minutes. "Gohain da says an *igu* is a witch doctor."

"Ask him if he knows anything about a *sahib* called Barrington," I asked, now really worried.

Gohain *da* suddenly looked at me as though he had seen a ghost. He pointed a finger at me and in a shrill voice said in Assamese (which I could understand quite well now) "Barrington was a *boga sahib*[25] …the butcher of Patharughat. He killed more than 140 innocent peasants here in this very place…did not even spare women and children. My grandfather and elder uncle died in the massacre[26]. They say…he had evil powers and no one could harm him."

---

[24]Respectful suffix in Bengali

[25]White *sahib*

[26]Refer trivia section for more details on the "Patharughat Massacre"

"When did he die and where is he buried?" I said with my voice on the edge of panic.

"*Sahib*, I don't know how that boga *sahib* died or where he is buried but it was finally the great Apatani[27] *igu* from the North who cursed him to damnation of hell…that is what my father told me when I was a kid!"

I knew I had to hurry and get the three to close the séance which now seemed like a really bad idea as we seemed to have woken up something we did not understand. I ran out of the house and towards the grave. Surprisingly the light bulb was off and it was dark.

I gingerly moved closer to the site and shone my torch. Noyon appeared slumped over the grave and the other two were sitting still. I was now really scared.

"Suchitra! Gohain *da*! Come over!" I shouted as I shook Chatterjee and Debu. They seemed in a daze and suddenly got up with a start.

"What the hell happened?" said Chatterjee.

"What's wrong with Noyon?" said Debu trying to wake up Noyon.

Suchitra and Gohain da too had fetched up along with another servant. Noyon too woke up looking pale and scared. We quickly picked up the Ouija boards, the sheets of paper and the rest of the things and quickly moved indoors.

"What the hell happened while I was gone?" I asked Chatterjee.

"I don't know…I can't remember," said Chatterjee.

Debu too nodded his head negatively.

Noyon had started shivering now and within an hour was wracked by high fever.

"104 deg F…need to get her to a doctor urgently," said Suchitra looking at the thermometer. "I wonder how she got this…she was up and about all this while. I told you people

---

[27]A tribe native to Arunachal Pradesh in India

not to meddle with planchet and stuff!"

In the meantime, I had called the Patharughat Police Station to trace any information on Barrington at Patharughat and Darrang.

Sen, the mild-mannered Estate doctor meanwhile arrived and examined Noyon.

"Saar, she's bad and we have to move her to the hospital at Darrang. Her fever is very high. We need to put some ice packs on her and move her out immediately."

The ice packs were brought and placed on Noyon's forehead. The fever did not subside even after one hour and Noyon appeared barely conscious. She also appeared to be delirious and was blabbering and mumbling incoherently. We could catch only a few words of what she was saying. "…I won't leave anyone…all will die!" which she repeated a number of times.

Chatterjee and Suchitra exchanged worried glances with me.

We then decided to move Noyon to Darrang Civil Hospital which was about an hour's drive. Luckily the weather was reasonably dry and Chatterjee along with Debu packed Noyon in a blanket in the rear seat of Chatterjee's lumbering Buick Roadmaster.

The car moved through the darkness and I followed it in my Jeep. Noyon was immediately moved to the emergency of the hospital. Her fever had still not gone down and she was getting more incoherent. The doctor administered her two injections and connected a drip. He told us not to worry and said that the fever should subside adequately in about an hour. Her fever did come down in an hour but the Doctor advised that it would be better if she were to spend the night in the hospital, so that he could keep her under observation.

Chatterjee decided to stay back in the hospital and requested me to drop Debu back at the Estate. After dropping off Debu and having a quick bite with him and Suchitra, I boarded my Jeep to head back to my quarters.

Suddenly, from nowhere old Gohain da emerged and gripping my forearm with surprising strength whispered "DSP *Sahib*! the evil *boga-sahib* is back. *Baudhi*[28] told me about the *jadu-tona*[29] you people did in the evening; and after that *didi*[30] became sick. I am sure the grave in the garden is of that evil man. God save us now!"

I could not sleep properly that night. Next morning, I drove to Darrang and checked out Noyon first. She seemed okay and was asleep. Then, I decided to run down to the Darrang Collectorate and check out a few things. I found Inspector Gogoi of Patharughat already there poring over some old documents.

"Sir, take a look at this…" he said thrusting an old yellowed leather-bound book towards me.

It was an old yearbook from the district archives dated from the turn of the 19th Century, which the book keeper had surprisingly found for us without much fuss. The yellowed pages were scrawled upon in neat yet archaic writing. It had enough information on Barrington. I spent the next hour and a half going through it, and then went back to Patharughat T.E. and had a detailed discussion with Gohain *da*.

What I inferred from the book and my conversation with Gohain *da* about Barrington was quite interesting. Samuel Barrington Esq, Imperial Police Service, was the SP of Darrang in the last decade of the 19th Century. It was during this time that the infamous *Patharughater Rann* or the Patharughat (as Patharughat was known then) Massacre took place. Barrington was unpopular, cruel and arrogant and treated natives with utter contempt. In 1894, when a group of emaciated peasants along with their families went to the District Magistrate (DM) to represent against the

[28]Elder sister

[29]Black magic

[30]Sister

absurdly high increase in taxes, Barrington had shooed them away after a sound thrashing though the DM was amicable enough to hear them out. This had enraged the villagers. One night, a group of about 200 villagers comprising of women and children gathered and marched to the *Dak Bungalow*[31] at Patharughat where the DM and SP were camping. Events took an ugly turn when the police party at the *Dak Bungalow* ill-treated the villagers. Enraged, a few elements from the mob pelted stones at the *dak bungalow* and there was talk of setting the place on fire. Without warning, a furious Barrington ordered the policemen to open fire at the motley crowd. In the ensuing firing ordered by the SP, at least 140 innocent villagers lost their lives. So evil and vindictive was Barrington, that he did not allow the kin of the deceased to even lift the bodies of their loved ones and let the bodies rot and be eaten by crows and dogs.

Two attempts on his life were made by revolutionaries seeking revenge. But, legend goes that he was a Devil worshipper who was able to fathom any plot against him and invariably put the plotters under heinous torture and atrocious depraved deaths.

It was at the insistence of village elders that a famous and powerful Shaman or *igu* of the primitive Apatani tribe from the North East Frontier Agency (N.E.F.A) was summoned at great effort and expense to put an end to the atrocities of Barrington. What happened after that is hazy…but they say that Barrington was found in a lifeless state with his eyes open, something akin to brain dead, one fine morning. It was legend that the *igu* had entrapped Barrington in a spell and locked him up in some unknown dimension. He had subsequently been buried in an unmarked grave.

Inferring from this strange tale, it seemed that in childish exuberance we had actually communicated with the evil

[31]Government rest house

undead spirit of Superintendent Barrington whose body was most probably buried in Chatterjee's garden.

I sat up with a jerk as the phone next to me rang shrilly. I was in the midst of probably my 10th cup of tea from the morning as I sat on the Inspector's desk at the Darrang Police Station, mulling over the notes I had made on what I had inferred so far.

It was the Doctor from the Hospital. He was just informing me that Noyon was now fine and was leaving the hospital with Chatterjee. I went to the hospital and found Chatterjee and Noyon waiting for me at the lobby. She looked a little pale but smiled at me.

"Ajay…thanks for everything. We are heading back home; the doc has given her a clean chit," said Chatterjee.

"Doctor, what was it that caused such high fever last night?" I asked the medical officer.

"Sir, it is quite strange; she's perfectly fine. All her vitals, blood reports and all other tests are normal. From this morning, she has been perfectly fine."

A few days passed uneventfully and I was embroiled in my day to day law and order chores and then got busy ensuring that on 26th January, the 45th Republic Day passed off peacefully.

It was on the evening of 28th January that I got a call from Chatterjee.

"Hi Ajay…free in the evening today, I hope. These kids are leaving for college tomorrow. They wanted to meet you. Can you come over for dinner?"

"Sure thing…I will be there at around 8:00 p.m. if it is okay," I confirmed.

I decided to give my driver a break and drove alone to the Estate House. The Chatterjees were their usual genial selves.

"How is Noyon feeling?" I asked Suchi.

"Why don't you ask her yourself young man…?" said Suchi with a wink.

"I am feeling perfect and don't feel like going back to the hustle and bustle of Calcutta..." declared Noyon, who looked stunning in a green chiffon sari. Even Debu looked reasonably presentable and washed.

The pleasant evening lingered on and the fine single malt and fish n chips made us all feel heady once again. The somewhat unpleasant events of the evening of my last visit were all but forgotten. A delicious dinner was then served by Suchi.

"Ummm...amazing food!" I declared. "Gohain da has outdone himself."

"Suchi and Noyon have crafted the menu today...Gohain da has taken the day off for his grandfather's *shradh*[32]. In fact, we sent off Dipankar also as he was required to be back here early morning tomorrow," said Chatterjee.

"Sorry ladies; and thanks for this wonderful spread," I said a tad embarrassed.

"Glad you like it..." said Noyon rather coyly.

It was getting cold and Chatterjee had activated the fireplace. We finished supper and were having a night cap as he poked the embers and put in some fresh dry twigs to keep the fire going.

It was past 1 a.m. when we decided to call it a night.

As I stood up to go Suchi said, "Ajay...it is late and cold. I suggest you tuck in at the guest room for the night. You can leave in the morning after breakfast. In fact, all of us are leaving for Guwahati to put Noyon and Debu on the train."

As I was drunk and tired, I readily accepted the offer and retired to the small yet cosy guest room. I fell asleep the moment I hit the bed.

It must have been a few hours later that I got up. I don't know what woke me up but I was feeling very thirsty. I looked around for the light switch but could not find it. I

[32]Death anniversary

went downstairs to find some water. I found a bottle of water on the dining table. After gulping down some water I pushed the curtains on the French windows to let some ambient light inside.

There was a row of yellow flickering lights outside. I rubbed my eyes to make sure I was not hallucinating. But indeed, the row of lights seemed to be moving closer. I opened the veranda door and went outside to check it out. A cold draught of wind greeted me as I stepped out on the lawn. It was quiet but for chirping of crickets and croaking of frogs. I could hear a dull mumbling sound from a distance and it appeared to be drawing closer. The row of lights which now appeared to be wooden torches with flames on top were also drawing closer. They were not a row of lights but a large number of them. My heart skipped a beat when I could roughly make out shapes of human figures carrying the torches approaching the house about 400-500 yards away, through the tea estate.

I heard a sound like foot falls to my left. It appeared as though a few people were also coming from the front and left of the house and moving in the direction of the tea estate. It was pitch dark but for the darting fire flies and the torches in the distance. The house too was pitch dark, even the security lights along the boundary and the bulb on the tree near Barrington's grave were off. Must be a damned power cut! I thought.

"Who's there?" I called out in Assamese in the direction in which I heard the footfalls.

There was no answer. The mob with the torches was now drawing closer and I could make out the shapes of the carriers of the torch. They were mostly bare torso, wearing *dhotis*[33] and many had a cloth tied on their heads like rough turbans. It all looked strangely old fashioned.

---

[33]Indian sarong

I could not take it anymore and decided to alert Chatterjee and Debu and also call up the police station for a back-up. As I turned to go towards the house, I heard a plaintive cry and someone from the group of people threw one of the wooden torches towards the house. The torch landed in the lawn near the location of Barrington's grave. I turned to look. My blood curdled as I saw in the dim flickering light that there was no grave below the tree – just the lawn extending up to the base!

I ran towards the house – my panic was real now. As I was looking in the direction of the old tree and running, I banged into someone or something!

I heard the person curse loudly in English, "Damn you! Can't you see where you are going…?"

The accent was clipped and unmistakably British.

I looked around in the darkness but could not find anybody. I finally reached the house and stood panting on the veranda totally disoriented. I was trying to locate the door in the darkness.

"Chatterjee, Debu where are you…Chatterjee!!" I yelled on the top of my voice. But there was no movement inside the house.

There was a commotion building up in the garden area as the mob had drawn closer; and now more than one flaming torch came flying through the air towards the house. A bush in the garden had caught fire. In the glare of the small fire I saw a group of 8-10 people in police uniform standing with old fashioned long barrelled muskets looking in the direction of the mob.

Who the hell are all these people I wondered and yelled out, "Hey! what is happening…who are you all?"

They did not seem to hear me and were talking to each other in a low voice. I again felt as though someone brushed past me; I fancied I got a slight whiff of a perfume which Noyon had worn the last evening.

"Noyon…is it you?" I called out.

There was no reply. I surely must be imagining things as it was all getting very unnerving now.

I decided enough was enough and walked towards the men in police uniform standing towards the far end of the lawn. Surprisingly in spite of the cold weather I was sweating profusely.

I stopped just short of the men, when I saw a uniformed, fair skinned, thickset man standing with the soldiers and speak in a highly anglicized Hindi, "Load up your muskets… let's teach these scoundrels a lesson."

I stood transfixed as though hypnotized. I opened my mouth to yell out but surprisingly no sound came out of my mouth. In abject terror, I hid myself behind the wooden partition in the veranda and watched the strange drama unfold in front of me. The soldiers quickly loaded their muskets and then there was a loud racket as 4-5 of the muskets went off together in the direction of the mob which was less than 50 yards from the boundary of the garden now. I could clearly see the figures now, but could hardly discern the faces as they appeared blurred – my eyes too seemed to be failing me now.

There were hideous cries as a number of the figures in the front line fell to the fusillade of the gun fire being brought down by the policemen. Another round of gunfire ensued and then another…till I lost track. I could hear the anglicized voice shout something else and then burst into a guttural laughter.

In spite of the volley being brought down by the policemen, the mob which must have outnumbered the former 30:1 had reached the garden and had now brought down most of the soldiers and were hacking them down with *daos*[34] or machetes. To my horror I realized that they were also trying to torch down the house. I saw one of the villagers rush up to the veranda with a flaming torch, but he fell as a

---

[34]Assamese machete

shot from the white man's pistol ripped through his back. The flaming torch fell on the Bougainvillea bush hugging the veranda and the former burst into flames. The dying middle aged man turned over in pain. His worn face quite resembled Gohain *da's* though different.

I decided that I must do something now, or else I as well as the others in the house would die. I moved out of my hiding place to the lawn when I saw a weird figure wearing something which looked like an ostrich's plume and a long ornate spear decorated with peacock feathers in his hand, wearing what looked like leopard skin and ash smeared on the face, chant something loudly in a strange language, impale the white man by driving the spear through his chest and then pulling it out.

The white man in khaki uniform yelled loudly as his dress got darkened by his life blood spurting out through the hole in his chest. Before I realized it, he ran towards me and collided squarely with me and both of us fell on the ground in the lawn.

"Help me…! Help me please…" the apparition said in a hoarse voice. The face was pale and the macabre eyes, sea blue in colour seemed to pierce through me.

I tried to push off the figure in utter fright and for all my bravado found myself wetting my pants. The figure in leopard skin had now drawn closer and charged once again at the white man with what looked like a stout baton topped by a human skull. The white man took the blow squarely on his head and with a choked scream slumped over my prone form once again.

My nerves gave way and I passed out.

"*Sahib*, *Sahib*!" I heard a distant voice call out.

I was not sure if I was alive. I opened my eyes and tried to focus. My head was throbbing badly. I saw the worried face of Inspector Gogoi looking down upon me.

"What happened Gogoi…? Where am I?" I asked

groggily trying to orient myself.

"Saar! It was horrible…the whole house burned down. The fire department people tell me that the fire was most probably due to the fire place not being extinguished completely at night. It was not properly maintained and so the embers must have spilled over to the wooden flooring of the room and set the whole place on fire."

I sat up with a jerk. I was on some kind of a hospital bed – probably the civil hospital. "Where are Chatterjees and their guests? The boy and the girl? And how did I get here?"

Gogoi looked very unhappy, "Sir there is nothing much we could do. By the time somebody informed us and help reached, Chatterjee *sahib*, *memsahib* and the boy were burned to death with the house…we found their badly charred bodies. But you and the girl miraculously escaped. You were lying unconscious in the garden and so was she some distance from you."

"Shit! Chatterjee, Suchi and Debu gone…died horrible deaths!" I said and suddenly recalled the hideous events I had witnessed last night.

"Where is the girl? Noyon?" I asked the Doctor who had by then come to my room.

"She was conscious but seemed off balance. We have sedated her. She is in Room No 6," he replied.

I was okay and the hospital let me off after a day's rest on the evening of 30th January. I decided to look up Noyon before I left the hospital. She was conscious but seemed in a stupor. Gohain da was sitting by her bedside. She must be in a state of severe shock I guessed, as she did not even seem to recognize me when I tried speaking to her. She just gave me a blank stare through her large eyes – *sea blue in colour* – they seemed strangely out of place on her face.

The Investigating Officer, an Inspector from the Darrang Police Station recorded my statement.

"It is an undoubted case of accident. Only you and that

girl got out on time, probably because both your rooms were closer to the exit. The Doctor tells me that you too must have inhaled quite a bit of the Carbon Monoxide, that's why you passed out. A little longer and both of you too would have probably not made it."

"Are you sure there was no deliberate sabotage, or somebody setting the house on fire from the outside?" I asked the Officer.

"I don't think so Sir... We got the forensics and the sniffer dogs to check out the complete area – not a single thing out of the ordinary indicating any deliberate sabotage to burn down the house. In fact, there was no one in the vicinity of the house, as even the servants were off duty at that point of time." he said quite confidently.

I decided to drive down to Patharughat TE and check out the site of the fire myself. I was horrified to find that what was once a beautiful piece of heritage property was now just a burnt-out shell. The beautiful home within, with all the wonderful people in it, and the pristine garden too, were all gone.

Just out of curiosity I glanced towards the grave. My heart skipped a beat as the grave suddenly seemed to be new and recently made. It was all the same as I had seen earlier – the slab, the tomb stone everything was identical – only it just did not seem that old anymore.

Gogoi dropped me off at my quarters and before I got down handed me over a brown paper bag.

"What is this?" I asked from curiosity.

"Oh, nothing sir! These are your soiled clothes and the things on your person at the time of the incident. The hospital gave it to return to you," said Gogoi.

As I picked up the bag it gave way from the bottom spilling its contents. Out fell my clothes neatly washed and ironed, my belt, socks and another small piece of cloth charred at the edges. The driver quickly switched on his flash light and started picking up the spilt contents. The beam of light fell on the small piece of khaki cloth which seemed stiffened by buckram. It appeared to be some kind of name tab. I didn't recall have one of this kind. I squinted to read what was written on it. It spelt "B A R R I N…" and the balance was charred. But I think I knew what the rest meant!

"Where did you find this?" I asked Gogoi.

"I don't remember exactly Sir…I think it was just struck to your clothes along with the mud and dirt when we picked you up from here.

Noyon never recovered from the incident and passed away in a lunatic asylum in Calcutta a couple of years later in spite of her parents' best efforts to have her treated. I kept track of her till her passing. The Doctors at the asylum told me that she had one of the severest cases of schizophrenia they had ever known and had in fact totally dissociated herself from her real identity and spoke incoherently about being trapped by an Igu (they didn't know what that meant) and her wanting to go back to England (where she had never been to earlier). I attended her funeral at the invitation of her grief-stricken parents. I also quietly consigned the somewhat charred little piece of buckram which was still with me, to her funeral pyre.

A year after the incident, Patharughat TE was taken over by a multinational company and the premises of the Estate House were razed to make way for a large tea processing plant. I too had by then moved out on promotion first to North Assam and thereafter on deputation to Delhi. I consciously never returned to Patharughat or Darrang ever again during my entire career.

Story **FIVE**

THE TATTOOED HAND

The oldest and strongest emotion of mankind is fear, and the oldest and strongest kind of fear is fear of the unknown.
-H. P. Lovecraft

14th March 2013

The day had begun as any other ordinary one. Ashok had left by the morning local from Kharghar to Wadala[35] where he worked in an accountancy firm. It was not that they could not afford a car or stay closer, but both Ashok and Malati had voluntarily decided to move out of the hustle and bustle of the polluted environs of Mumbai, to this distant yet pristine suburb.

[35]Localities in Mumbai

The local was surprisingly full today, even the First-Class coach in which he travelled. The train reached Vashi and a horde of commuters rushed into the train. There was practically no place to even stand; and a few of them hung out dangerously from the door.

"These guys are nuts. Really surprising to see educated people behave like this," Ashok wondered looking apprehensively at the passengers hanging on the foot board.

After about an hour and 15 minutes, he realized that the train had crossed GTB Nagar Railway station and would be reaching his destination very soon. He got up from his seat and gingerly made his way up to the door. There was still quite a rush in the train. He moved closer to the door and waited there flipping through his WhatsApp messages on his mobile. Suddenly, he felt a violent force trying to snatch his laptop bag. He held on hard and tried to locate the snatcher in the crowd.

Suddenly, he felt a stinging sensation in his hand gripping the bag and then someone pushed him hard.

Ashok fell out of the moving train on the tracks. As the train was slowing down, the impact was not much and he fell on a grassy patch. More than the impact, it was the shock of the whole turn of events which numbed him. What happened after, was that in a nightmarish stupor he saw people in the slowed down train furiously motion to him about something. Before he could realize what happened he felt a terrible pain in his arms and a roaring noise behind him. He then passed out.

"Ashok! Ashok! Can you hear me!" he could hear a vaguely familiar voice call out seemingly at the end of a tunnel since it resonated surreally into his brain. He opened his eyes and saw the blurred image of Malati's tear stained face peering anxiously at him.

He looked up. He tried to sit up but the paramedic and doctor next to him restrained him.

"Thank God you woke up! I thought you'll die and leave

me all alone!" blurted Malati breaking into tears. Trying to console her Ashok tried to lift his right arm and a searing pain ran through his body. He looked down and was horrified to see what appeared to be stumps in place of his complete arms covered with a bloodied bandage, dipped in an ice pack.

"What happened to me? Where are my hands? What happened to me?" he said repeatedly, first in a whisper and then later in a shrill scream.

The Doctor calmed him down and gave him an injection which made him drift off into a fitful drug induced stupor. The next few days passed in a trance like state with fleeting images of a sobbing and weary Malati, a kindly elderly doctor looking down upon him, strobe lights similar to those on a surgeon's table (he vaguely remembered seeing them in some movie).

5th April 2013

He woke up finally after an undefined time period and opened his eyes, still feeling drowsy. He again saw Malati's face staring at him anxiously. She seemed to have aged all of a sudden. He really could not remember much all of a sudden. Where am I…? Looks like a hospital…what am I doing here?" his still sub conscious mind wondered.

"Ashok!! Are you okay…?" he heard Malati's voice ask him.

Surprisingly he was able to mumble a reply, "Yes…I am fine. What happened to me?"

One or two more days passed in his recuperation. He was able to now orally take fluids and slowly began gaining strength and finally began to get oriented.

"Darling! You are God's miracle. You fell off the train and got badly injured," said Malati still looking a tad woebegone.

The surreal dream like images of the past few days (or months?) flashed in front of his eyes all of a sudden and he got up with a start. "Shit! I think I lost my hands…" he thought, recalling the blood-soaked bandages on the stumps of his arms, doused in an ice pack. He looked down upon his arms. They were still covered in bandages with small blood stains but his hands seemed intact, though they felt kind of strange.

Then Malati recounted a most amazing story.

Yes…he had lost both his hands when a train in the opposite track ran them over amputating them just above the wrist joint. His amputated hands though immediately taken in an ice box by some alert bystander to the hospital, were too damaged and contaminated to be put back.

His employers Dorabjee & Co. Chartered Accountants, had him shifted to Lilavati Hospital for the best treatment. As luck would have it Professor Nadey Hakim the famous US-Lebanese transplant surgeon was visiting Mumbai and on request of Dr Kothari, the principal orthopaedist of Lilavati Hospital, he checked out Ashok. Mr. Nuserwan Dorabjee the owner of Dorabjee & Co. was quite fond of Ashok and looked upon him as one of the bright sparks of the future. He was able to impress upon Prof Hakim to try and attempt a transplant on Ashok. But where was a donor to donate hands…? And such a surgery had been performed only a very few times in the world. The only solace was that Prof Hakim had been part of most of the successful ones done in the recent past.

Though Ashok had been unlucky with the accident, luck seemed to be favouring him otherwise, as the hospital was able to line up a compatible donor within a day. This too was a rarity since the 'donor' hand usually comes from a brain-dead donor. Hand transplants are a new category of transplants where multiple organs are transplanted as a single functional unit, termed 'Vascularized Composite Allotransplantation' or VCA. The operation was quite extensive and lasted 10 hours. (By comparison, a typical heart transplant operation lasts 6 to 8 hours). The team of surgeons led by Prof Hakim connected the bones first, followed by tendons, arteries, nerves, veins, and skin. Thankfully Ashok's body had accepted the donor's hands, again a 50-50 chance usually, and his wounds were healing nicely.

Amazed by the unbelievable story Ashok looked down at his 'new' hands. They were a tad darker than his 'original' hands and slightly bigger. But had some strange makings at the edges, something similar to henna markings and a small tattoo in a script he could not understand on the right hand.

His inquiring looks had Malati smiling, "Don't worry they are okay. It is just that your benefactor probably used *mehendi*[36] on his hands for quite a few years and therefore the marks are almost permanent. In any case his identity is secret, so I don't know who it was and I do not want to know. Only I will thank the poor soul for the rest of my life for giving you his hands."

"Did you tell Appa I'm in hospital?" asked Ashok.

"Yes, I did," replied Malati shaking her head negatively. "You don't worry…I am there for you…for all time." She cuddled him and comforted him seeing the disappointed look on his face.

Ashok's parents – his father and step-mother, had severed all ties with him since the time had had got married to Malati, his classmate from college. She was bright, pretty and full of life; but an orphan and a divorcee at the time of her marriage to Ashok. Ashok's father Ram Shetty was a prominent hotelier. It had been five years now, and apart from an occasional phone call there was no contact between the couple and Ashok's parents. His father had legally disowned Ashok, his only son, from all his inheritance and in turn transferred the same to his second wife.

10th May 2013

Long sessions of physio-therapy saw Ashok's new hand functions almost restored to normal. Initially he felt a little

[36]Henna

strange since there was a distinct colour difference between his arm and hands but then he was more or less used to this oddity. Ashok was discharged and certified fully fit to resume normal duties. He joined back at work and he and Malati tried to put all that had transpired behind them and resume normal life.

17th May 2013

The first week at work had passed off well. His colleagues had ensured that he did not have too much of backlog considering that he was non-operational for almost 3 ½ months. Malati was traveling out of town on official work for a few days and Ashok was all alone at home once he got back from work.

He was still uneasy about the fact that he did not know whose hands he was using now. He had repeatedly inquired with the hospital and the police but had been politely declined saying that the law did not permit revealing the identity of the donor in this case.

Ashok looked at the small tattoo on his hand and decided that he must decipher what was written there. It was definitely an oriental script. He Googled various scripts and found the Thai script to be the nearest match. He quickly opened the Thai alphabet and tried to decipher the written word – it roughly translated to *Nilofer*.

"Seems to be somebody's name," he wondered. It sounded vaguely familiar. "In any case what does it mean…?" he thought aloud and absent-mindedly Googled it. It threw up about 14,40,000 results in 0.61 seconds!

Out of the top 10 results 8 were about Nilofer Bano. *Nilofer Bano*! Of course, I know who it is! Nilofer Bano was one of the most infamous serial killers of recent times. She was a eunuch who used to abduct and kill small children, horribly mutilating them in the process. The story was that she used to follow cannibalistic tantric rituals. A huge nationwide manhunt had been launched and she had finally been nabbed about a year back.

"*Nilofer Bano Hanged to Death in Arthur Road Jail: Parents of Victims finally get Closure*" screamed a headline in "*The Indian Express*" of 1st April 2013. He read the news item. It spoke of the psychotic transgender, a big name in the city's underworld child and woman trafficking trade who had ruthlessly murdered at least 12 people with her own hands with her preferred weapon, a meat cleaver. The law finally caught up with Nilofer as one of the victims managed to escape and was able gather enough courage to describe her to the police. His curiosity tickled further, he opened up another detailed report in the *Times of India.* It described in detail how the police had tracked and finally zeroed down upon the killer. The evidence which clinched it was, the escaped victim's testimonial and also a CCTV footage of Nilofer drawing money from an ATM near one of the crime scenes. The report went on to say that the footage had revealed that the killer had henna design and a small tattoo on her right hand, similar to what had been described by the child.

Ashok's heart froze…he now refined the Google search and typed 'nilofer bano tattoo'. Lo and behold! The search threw up another few thousand results. He gingerly clicked on the images. He was now sweating profusely in spite of the cool weather. The first image which opened made him exclaim and almost fall off the chair…and instinctively look down on his right hand. It was a perfect match! He ran to the bedroom and opened his cupboard to fetch his medical documents. He flipped through them and finally located the documents pertaining to his surgery. His blood ran cold. The time and date of his transplant was 4 p.m., 1st April 2013. He ran back to the computer and tracked the time and date of Nilofer's hanging- it was 5 a.m., 1st April 2013! Nilofer's body had been buried at an unknown location since she had no known relatives or next of kin, just a fellow Eunuch, Shabnam was present for the burial.

Ashok was ravenous with hunger and went to the kitchen to fix up a snack. Something glinted in the kitchen as he switched on the light. It was the big meat cleaver which Malati used to cut up the chicken into smaller pieces. The cleaver hung there as it always did. But today it seemed to have a different attraction to him. He went up to it and picked it up and swung it in the air in a slashing movement.

After a hurried snack, he fell into a fitful sleep. He got up with a start sweating profusely. His mobile was ringing. It was Malati.

"Hi Malati! How are you?" he answered groggily. It was 11 p.m. at night.

"Why didn't you call? Are you okay?" said the voice at the other end sounding worried.

"I am okay. Just a hectic day at office. I just crashed out," said Ashok. He did not tell her about his discovery of the evening. "She's already had a tough last three months. I should not make her worry more," decided Ashok.

"I will be back in another 3 days. You just cheer up," said Malati before hanging up. He fell into slumber once again.

Something again woke him up. He checked the mobile. It said 2 a.m. He was feeling uneasy and went to the kitchen for a glass of water. The cleaver glinted evilly at him. As though hypnotized he picked up the cleaver. He was feeling warm all of a sudden and decided to take a walk down stairs to get some fresh air. He took the lift and went down to the common park. There was not a single soul in sight. Just the watchman dozing on his chair. Suddenly a rage possessed him and with a growl he swung the cleaver (which incidentally he had carried with him) and slashed at the guard. The sleeping man did not have a chance. Ashok thereafter repeatedly slashed him till he was all bloodied and very dead. Suddenly a ringing sound went off…something like a burglar alarm. The sound seemed to shake him out of this murderous stupor. He looked around and suddenly the watchman, the park and other things seemed to vanish. He was in his bed and the alarm on his mobile was ringing. It was 6 a.m.

"Oh God! Am I going mad or have I been possessed by the evil Nilofer!"

He ran to the kitchen to look for the cleaver, but found it hanging neat and clean as he had left it after dinner. He called the security room on the intercom thereafter and anxiously inquired about the night guard. He was relieved to learn that the man had finished his duty and gone home.

Last week of May 2013

The next few days passed off with Ashok getting absurd visions of violent crimes and the meat cleaver haunted him so much that he picked it up and put it into the lower drawer so that it was out of his sight. Thankfully Malati was back as scheduled.

The moment she saw him, she gasped, "Ashok! What's wrong with you? You look awful!"

Not wanting to alarm her, he just told her that he was having problems sleeping and the lack of sleep had made him look haggard.

It was not only at home but at work too, that people noticed changes in his behaviour. He was lagging behind in his work and Mr. Dorabjee had already counselled him albeit gently for mistakes created in the accounts of two prestigious clients.

On the insistence of Malati, Ashok finally agreed to meet Dr Kothari again. Finally, in front of Dr Kothari and Malati he blurted out as to how he had come to know that his new hands were the hands of a psychotic killer and how he was tortured by the presence of the cleaver, just like the one used by the killer. He now believed that along with the hands he has acquired the murderer's predisposition to violence.

He broke down and sobbed, "Why didn't you tell me whose hands these were? I would have never agreed. Please remove them…I am scared for Malati and all the things I love. I feel my hands are not in my control anymore."

The kindly surgeon looked at him and said in a quiet voice, "Son! I am sorry you came to know all this. I possibly could not tell you since I was bound by law. But believe me a person's acts are not governed by hands, but by the head and heart. There is nothing wrong with you. It is only the shock of the discovery combined with all the physical and mental trauma you have undergone for the last few months that is playing games on your mind. Let me refer you to Dr Mehta, he is a very good Psychiatrist and a dear friend. He will help you."

"Doctor *sahib* you don't understand! I am not mad…I am *possessed*! Please help me!" said Ashok not convinced. But finally, a sedative injection and some more convincing by Dr Kothari saw Ashok calm down a little and see reason. The couple drove back home in silence.

10th June 2013

A few visits to Dr Mehta saw a marginal improvement in his countenance to the situation. However, professionally, his work continued to suffer as he somehow could not convince himself to work with his new hands on his accountancy. He simply started making too many mistakes and it was costing the firm a great deal of reputation. Finally, Mr. Dorabjee called Ashok and very politely told him that he needed to take a break. He was willing to give him leave without pay for as long as he wanted but in his present condition he had no option but to ask him to discontinue coming to work forthwith. Mr. Dorabjee was ill at ease and genuinely felt for Ashok – but he had a business to run after all.

15th August 2013

The current predicament did not help Ashok's cause at all.

The anti-depressant drugs combined with alcohol made a deadly cocktail and he became moodier and more melancholy as the days went by. The last straw was when Malati who had a modest job as a data operator in a telecom firm, was also laid off by her employers as part of a 'manpower rationalization' drive. In spite of their best efforts, neither of them was able to get another job even after 2 months.

With debts piling up and no source of income, the bank had already issued a notice for the house loan as they had defaulted the last two payments.

Malati finally told him, "Ashok, I think you must speak to your father to help us out. After all you are his only son!"

Ashok mulled over it. It was their only option, though he reviled at the thought of approaching his father. Seeing his face, Malati said "C'mon cheer up! You must go and meet him tomorrow!"

Accordingly, Ashok SMS-ed his father stating that he wanted to meet him the next evening at 6:00 p.m.

He got a curt "OK make it at 8" as a reply.

16th August 2013

The next day Ashok left home at 6:00 p.m. and took the fast train to Santa Cruz from where he took a cab to reach their plush family mansion at Juhu. Surprisingly, there was no one at the gate. He reached the front door and reached out and rang the bell. Seeing that the door was slightly open he pushed and went in. There didn't seem to be any body there.

"*Appa*![37] Are you there? It's me Ashok!" said Ashok looking around.

He saw the bed room door to open and he went in. The things in the room were in disarray and there appeared to have been a struggle which had taken place there. The white bed sheet seemed to be stained with something dark at the

[37]Father

far end. He gingerly moved forward. He froze at the sight which greeted him. His father was lying on the floor facing the roof and in a pool of blood. He definitely was very dead; his blank fixed eyes and frozen horror-stricken face told it all. Lying next to him was the murder weapon, a blood-stained meat cleaver!

"This seems to be similar to what we have at home..." he wondered.

Panic stricken Ashok ran out of the room and the house which surprisingly still appeared to be sans any occupant barring his dead father. Ashok ran on the road outside and hailed a cab. He was sweating profusely and asked the driver to take him home. He couldn't not bear it anymore. He cupped his face in his hands and began sobbing. But suddenly he stopped and looked down at his hands.

"You have ruined me Nilofer! What is happening to me. I am going mad!"

The cab driver got alarmed and stopped the cab by the road side. "Anything the matter *sahib*?" he inquired in a worried tone.

"Nothing, just drop me home," replied Ashok.

The rest of the journey was uneventful.

The moment Malati opened the door and saw his face, she sensed something was wrong. "What happened Ashok? You look like shit!"

Ashok ran to the kitchen and opened the second drawer to check if the cleaver was where he had placed it. It was not there!

"Did you take out the meat cleaver from here?" he asked Malati.

"No! I did not. In fact, I was looking around for it after you went as I was planning to make some chicken tonight. But what the hell has happened?" she asked again.

Ashok told her the entire turn of events. Shocked to silence, Malati helped Ashok search the whole house for the cleaver. Surprisingly, it was not there anywhere!

"I told you my hands are out of control...did I do it?" sobbed Ashok.

"Don't be silly! I only sent you off in the morning. You definitely were not carrying the cleaver," comforted Malati.

"We must inform the police immediately...I did nothing... and how mercilessly have they killed Appa!" lamented Ashok.

Just than the doorbell rang startling both of them.

There was a youngish looking police inspector with two male and one female constable standing outside the door. "Are you Ashok Shetty?" he asked curtly.

Ashok nodded affirmatively.

"Take him into custody" he directed the constable, who promptly slipped a handcuff on Ashok.

"But, but...he has done nothing. What is his crime?" said a distraught Malati.

"He's wanted for the murder of Mr. Ram Shetty, his father. I can't tell you anything more. I am Inspector Patil and I am taking him to Juhu Police Station."

"But officer, you cannot take him away like that. We have rights!" said Malati trying to pull Ashok.

"Listen lady, just cut out the Hollywood crap. I'll book you too for obstruction of justice," he told her in an annoyed tone and motioned the female constable, who grabbed Malati's arm and took her inside the house as the other two cops took Ashok away.

Malati quickly took the car and rushed to Juhu Police Station. She couldn't think of anyone to call so she called Ashok's close friend and school mate, Nikhil, a lawyer by profession and also Dr Kothari. It emerged that an anonymous phone had tipped off the police about the murder of Ram Shetty. When the police reached the house, Geeta Shetty, Ashok's step mother was already there and sobbing inconsolably. She had told the police that she was out of the house for 2 hours for a kitty party at a friend's house when someone had come and murdered her husband. The gate CCTV footage of the time had shown only Ashok coming in and then running away. She was able to recognize him.

The inspector questioned Ashok, who said that his father was already dead by the time he had got there. Just then a constable entered with a piece of paper. Patil looked at it and nodded.

"Mr. Ashok, it is time you confessed, otherwise we have other means of finding it out. The fingerprint report has come. The fingerprints on the cleaver red-flagged immediately in our database because they are of the most infamous ones in recent times…Nilofer Bano; and you may not know it, but I have been told that you have been transplanted her hands."

Ashok broke down completely and started sobbing looking at his hands. Dr Kothari had reached by then and he intervened.

"Inspector, this man is not well and he is my patient. I know him well. He could never have done it."

"No Dr *sahib*! I told you my hands are out of my control. I don't know how it happened. I don't remember anything other than what I just narrated…but it is still Nilofer's hand which did it!" shrieked Ashok and then he passed out.

17th August 2013

Ashok woke up on a hospital bed and found poor Malati and Nikhil looking down at him along with Inspector Patil and Dr Kothari.

"I am leaving two policemen to guard your room Mr. Ashok. Please don't try anything funny. I will come back for the rest of the questioning once the Doctor permits me."

Ashok looked inquiringly at Malati and Nikhil.

Malati hesitatingly said, "Ashok, our maid has identified the murder weapon as ours and Geeta Shetty has hired an expensive lawyer to make a water tight case."

Nikhil continued, "But you don't worry. For the time being you'll be in hospital under police custody until your condition improves. That gives us some time to make a viable defence. Just wrack your brains and tell me anything else you remember."

30th August 2013

The motley crowd was chit-chatting in the court room and all rose when the Judge, Ramesh Tahiliani took his seat. He motioned them to sit down. The first hearing of this relatively high-profile case had come up. The court room soon filled up with more people and press men. This case was unique in recent times, it not only involved fratricide but even medical ethics were being questioned by the press, now that everyone was aware that Ashok had been transplanted Nilofer's hands.

The prosecution brought out a very water tight case with evidence of the maid who identified the knife, the CCTV footage which showed him clearly entering the house at 7:50 p.m. and exiting at 8:15 p.m. Ashok's step mother was looking smug rather than sad considering that her husband had been brutally murdered sometime back.

Nikhil took up defence on the plea that Ashok had undergone severe trauma both physically and mentally over the past number of months; and neither had the motive nor the inclination to commit the murder. However, his argument was not convincing as the evidence seemed ominously piled up against Ashok. Citing Ashok's medical condition, he was able to take 2 weeks' time from the police during which Ashok would be in the psychiatric ward of the Government Hospital under police protection.

"I must come up with something out of the box to crack this. I somehow cannot but help believe Ashok and Malati on this account. But the knife and the finger prints seem to clinch it for the prosecution," thought Nikhil wryly.

6:00 P.M., 2nd September 2013

The sewage was overflowing from the open drain and the stench was quite unbearable. Nikhil had used his sources to fix up a meeting with Yamuna Bai the maid who worked at Ashok's house. There had been something not right about her shifty eyes the other day at court, but he could not prove anything on that day. He therefore wanted to check her out face to face once. Her modest hut was in the heart of Dharavi. She called him into the dingy house and quickly shut the door. She had been unwilling to meet him, but a handsome tip passed on through the source had made her more willing to interact.

She was a widow with two grown up children whom she was trying to put through vocational courses at the local ITI[38]. Nikhil asked her generally about Ashok and Malati and the maid was all praises for their good behaviour and generosity towards her and said that she could not believe that the *sahib* could have done such a thing. Nikhil's meeting lasted for over an hour and he emerged from the hut appearing to be reasonably satisfied, and Yamuna Bai definitely appeared more ill at ease than before the meeting.

Nikhil's next halt was the Moonlight Dance Bar at Malad, a coordinate which had been provided by Yamuna Bai after a lot of coercion and financial persuasion.

"This is turning out easier than I thought. But the next stage may not be so smooth. I better line up Patil's team just in case there is some action."

He called up Inspector Patil and spoke to him briefly. He then locked his car and went up to the bar, the gates of which were guarded by two formidable looking bouncers. Smiling at them he went in. He went up to the bar and ordered a beer.

"Where can I find Shabnam?" he asked the waiter.

The waiter gave a blank look. A 500 Rupee note did the

---

[38]Vocational training institute

trick and he motioned to a red coloured door at the other end of the room, beyond the round stage where over made up women dressed in garish salwar kameez gyrated to raunchy Bollywood numbers.

The barman led him to the door and took him inside. There was another door which looked like that of a changing room and he lightly knocked at the door.

"Come in!" said a gruff voice.

Both of them entered the room. In the dim light Nikhil could see a huge form clad in a bright orange sari.

"Yes! Peter what is it?" she asked the bar tender.

"This man wants to meet you…says it's urgent!" said Peter hesitatingly.

"It better be urgent and important…I don't meet anyone," said Shabnam who had turned towards them by now.

Shabnam was one of the ugliest eunuchs Nikhil had seen in a long time. Fat, and with a bloated face with liver spots ringed blood shot eyes, made to look more hideous by the garish make-up. She squinted at him as though trying to recollect his face.

"Yes…who are you?" she growled.

Before Nikhil could reply she finally seemed to place him and her face contorted with rage. "You are that lawyer on that murder case…the one who killed with Nilofer's hands…I told them Nilofer cannot die, she will return." She snarled and continued, "Who allowed you here…? That bastard Peter must have taken money from you…get out of here! I know nothing about the case!"

"I know you know everything! I cannot let an innocent man be punished for what he has not done. I promise you I will make sure you are let off leniently if you turn approver," said Nikhil in a calm voice.

With a loud yell the eunuch lunged at Nikhil who fell down under the impact of the bulk. The eunuch's mobile to fell on the floor and started ringing. Nikhil was able to steal a glance at the caller's name – 'Geeta Madam' before Shabnam struck him across the face with a glancing blow.

Just then the door of the room opened and the room was flooded with light. Thankfully Inspector Patil and his team had reached on time. His pistol drawn he shouted at the eunuch to stand up. With a roar the eunuch pushed him aside and tried to rush out of the room. However, the two burly constables accompanying the inspector were able to hold her and prevent her from running out. The woman constable with the team slapped Shabnam across her face and the others two policemen promptly handcuffed her.

September-October 2013

The investigation into the case progressed rapidly after the clinching evidence presented by Nikhil. The chilling conspiracy hatched by Geeta Shetty was the stuff of a Bollywood potboiler.

It emerged that Ram Shetty was in a mood to reconcile with his estranged son and daughter in law. With an aim to get him out of the way, Geeta Shetty hired a petty criminal Sattar to kill Ashok by pushing him out of the train. Unfortunately for her, Ashok survived. When she came to know that his hands had been amputated and a donor was being sought, she realized that a well-known murderer with known fingerprints was being hanged; she used her influence to smoothly organize the transplant of hands of Nilofer to Ashok. Then she got in touch with Shabnam who was Nilofer's friend, through whom, she obtained the palm prints of Nilofer and got latex gloves with the prints made. She also made sure that information about Ashok never really trickled in fully to his father; and it was in fact she who took Malati's call and told her that Ram did not want to speak to Ashok.

She then was able to glean clinical information from Dr Mehta under the pretext of being Ashok's step mother and his insecurities and fears regarding his hands and his morbid attraction to a particular meat cleaver. She was able to organize the cleaver to be taken out from Ashok's house through the maid (who was threatened by Shabnam and thereafter paid some money).

Her influence was also used to make sure that both Ashok and Malati lost their jobs and things became easier when Ashok approached Ram seeking his assistance. She first got herself enough alibis by going off to a social gathering, and also sent off the servants for the evening; and the lone watchman at the gate was suddenly taken sick after eating his usual dinner which was provided from the bungalow.

Shabnam had entered through the backyard wicket gate and entered the house with the pass key provided by Geeta wearing the latex gloves with Nilofer's finger prints and the cleaver stolen from Ashok's house. Ram Shetty did not stand a chance against the big eunuch who ruthlessly murdered him with the cleaver, making sure he left plenty of finger prints all around. This happened at 7:30 p.m., just 15 minutes before Ashok came.

15 November 2013

In a landmark judgment, Ashok was acquitted in the case by the trial court and Shabnam and Geeta were taken into custody to be tried for criminal conspiracy and murder. Finally, Dr Kothari's words seemed to ring true that a person's acts are not governed by hands, but by the head and heart.

17 November 2013

Nikhil reached Ashok and Malati's place at around 8:00 p.m. The couple had invited him for dinner. Ashok opened the door of the apartment and Nikhil settled down on the drawing room sofa after taking off his shoes.

"Nikhil! You never told us how you got the lead regarding Shabnam!" said Ashok. "Well it all started when I saw the forensic report which specified that the murder had been done by a right-handed murderer. Nilofer was probably right handed but I definitely know that you are a leftie and found out that Shabnam was right handed too. The configuration of the hands is controlled by the brain and it cannot change even if the hands are transplanted. The left hand prints too were there in quite a few places but not too many on the murder weapon. The cleaver was identified by the maid and I realized that probably she was our first lead and could be the one who took it out of the house. It was a long shot, but luckily it was spot on!" replied Nikhil.

"Really! Did she tell you everything during your first meeting?" asked Ashok getting more interested.

"She denied everything at first but then a little persuasion, coercion and monetary compensation with a promise to keep her immunized from prosecution finally worked and she told me all about Geeta and Shabnam. By the way where is Malati…? Just fix me a drink too bro," said Nikhil.

"Malati has just gone down to the store…why don't you go into the dining room and make yourself a drink, while I rustle up a snack for us," said Ashok from the kitchen.

Nikhil went to the dining room and picked up a whisky bottle from the bar. The TV was playing out the news. A lot of coverage about their case. Nikhil felt really smug. All this publicity was going to help him professionally quite a bit. He had already got a number of congratulatory calls from all the top lawyers and some other important people in town.

He was flipping through the channels when Times Now suddenly flashed breaking news "Prime Witness in Ram Shetty murder case found brutally murdered". It showed the visual of Yamuna Bai's badly slashed blood-soaked body with the face blurred. But he could make out that it was her from the location (her house) and her tearful son who was making a statement.

"Ashok! Did you see this? It is horrible!" said Nikhil in a shocked voice.

He turned around to look for Ashok. But he was not in the kitchen.

"Ashok! Where are you? Someone killed Yamuna Bai!" he said turning towards the bedroom as he heard water flowing in the washroom. He entered the bedroom and tripped over something in the dim light. It was a human leg! To his horror he realized that it was Malati lying prone on the floor. The wash room door suddenly opened and out stepped Ashok. But there was something hideously wrong with him. He was dressed in a sari and had garish makeup on his face.

"What the hell is happening here?" he demanded.

"Nothing sweetheart!" said Ashok in a hoarse outlandish voice and clapped his hands in characteristic *hijra*[39] fashion. "You saved Ashok with that fantastic story you wove... but you should not have proved that poor Shabnam was the murderer. She was all I had. Shetty was already dead by the time she got there. Now she will hang because of you," continued the voice which definitely was not that of Ashok.

"Who...who are you?" said Nikhil utterly shocked.

Clicking his tongue Ashok continued "So you don't recognize me now! You should know...*Nilofer can never die*!"

Nikhil tried to run from the room but the looming form of Ashok blocked the door and drew a big knife in his left hand and slashed Nikhil across the chest.

"You missed out just one detail in the trial...I am not right or left-handed...I am ambidextrous! And only Shabnam knew about it!" screamed the figure before giving one last purposeful plunge of the knife with its right hand into Nikhil's chest and piercing his heart.

[39]Eunuch

Story **SIX**

THE TWO RUPEE DEBT

First our pleasures die - and then our hopes, and then our fears - and when these are dead, the debt is due dust claims dust - and we die too.
-Percy Bysshe Shelley

The journey from Trichy[40] to Madras[41] was getting boring. It was thirty years before today and the highway was without any of the fancy food courts, pizzerias and the likes. In fact, it was a two-lane road in those days, poorly lit and quite desolate, barring an occasional truck, considering that it was two hours past midnight. The old Morris Minor had no AC (like most cars

[40]Tiruchirappalli
[41]Current day Chennai

in those days) but the cool breeze wafting through the open quarter glass was adequate to keep us comfortable. Uncle Siva was maintaining a steady 70 kmph speed and the old car was quite comfortable doing that. Uncle Siva just loved to drive and he was actually very good at it. He was rock steady and alert as a blood hound even after driving continuously for about 3 ½ hours now.

"Uncle, how much more time will it take to reach Madras?" I asked him shifting my cramped limbs.

"Let me see, about 15 minutes to Villupuram and another three and a half hours from there. You know I was born near this place and spent my childhood here. But it is all changed now and it has been a long while since we shifted to Madras," replied Uncle Siva. "Anyways, haven't you slept?" he continued in an amused tone.

As a matter of fact, I was very tired having hardly slept or taken rest for the last three days attending Aunt Sita's wedding.

Sita was my mother's youngest sister and we had all gone to Trichy to attend her wedding. Dad and Mom had left directly for Bangalore after attending the main function as Dad did not get adequate leave. He was an Indian Police Service officer presently posted with the Vigilance Department in Bangalore. I decided to go along with Uncle Siva to Madras and spend my school holidays there with him. Uncle Siva was a widower who had lost his wife, Aunt Lakshmi two years earlier in a Rail accident. Everything about him was about strength and confidence and a never say die attitude. He had bounced back strongly from his personal tragedy and though one of the youngest of his generation, was one of the most respected members of our family, and definitely, my favourite Uncle.

"Uncle, I am not feeling sleepy and am bored. Why don't you tell me a story while you drive?" I replied with a yawn playing with some loose change kept in the ash tray beside the seat. There were 11 Rupees in 1 Rupee and 50 Paisa coins which I had counted over and over again to keep myself busy through the boring journey.

"What kind of story Muthu?" asked Uncle Siva.

"Ummm... a nice spooky Ghost Story!" I replied cheekily.

"Well, that's a good idea. But wont you get scared...? It is actually a dark night outside," said Uncle.

"Uncle, I am not scared. I am a policeman's son," I said, my pride hurt a little.

"Yes, of course! I forgot that you were the brave one!" he said in a bemused tone. "I think you deserve a really scary story and a true one."

"Real one? You mean it actually happened!" I said a tingle of thrill coursing through my veins.

"Hah,hah, hah...! Got you interested, didn't I?" said my uncle with a wink of his eye. "Well, here I go!"

"It happened long ago when I was still at school in Perangiyur (it was my maternal grandfather's native village). It was raining hard and the Then-Pennai River which flowed north of the village was full. My father had organized Math tuitions for me from Krishna Iyer, the genial Brahmin tutor who lived in Athiyur a small village across the river. Usually, I used to return from his place at around 4 p.m., but on that particular day I got late (by village standards). It was around 8 p.m. by the time I reached the *ghat*[42]. Thankfully it was not raining, but I could not find a single boatman there who could ferry me across the swollen river. All the boatmen who ferried people across had left for the night. Not a soul was to be found. I waited for 30 minutes before deciding that I'd return back to my tutor's place and spend the night there. But at that moment, I saw this lone boatman at a distance mooring his boat to a makeshift bollard. I called out to him and requested him to drop me across. Surprisingly, he agreed immediately to take me across for Two Rupees, as he said

[42]Jetty or place on a river bank for bathing or boarding boats

that he had been planning to go to the other side anyways in some time. I could hardly see his face in the darkness but could make out that he had a thick beard. I slid into the boat and he silently pulled it across the river, with only the sound of the oars splashing in the water for company. We reached across in about 10 minutes. As I got off the boat, I realized that I had left my bag on it. I also pulled out two rupees to pay the boatman. I turned around only to find my bag lying on the ground, entirely wet. I suddenly felt a chill and started shivering. I realized that I too was totally drenched to the bone as though I had taken a dip in the river waters. I frantically looked around. There was no boat or boatman anywhere around."

Uncle Siva paused for the punch line of the story to settle in.

I was frankly horror stricken and could only utter in a scared tone "Ddd...did this really happen to you?"

I think Uncle Siva decided that it was enough. "Hah, hah, hah relax Muthu, it was a long while ago and I was actually happy, since the Two Rupees I saved that night added to my pocket money substantially. I don't believe that there are any ghosts in any case! Why don't you get some sleep!" said uncle Muthu, his amused tone back.

Suddenly the car jerked and a whistling sound emanated from the rear right side.

"Shit! I think we have a flat. Why don't you help me Muthu? Let's just fix the spare tyre," said Uncle Siva stopping the car and getting down.

The road was pitch dark, with not a single soul in sight. Honestly, I was actually feeling very scared but Uncle Muthu's crisp voice commanded me once again to help him with the jacks. I groggily got down from the car and limbered up to the rear side of the car to find uncle already on the job. He took put the spare wheel and rolled it up to the right side of the car.

"Muthu, just hold the torch and shine it on the wheel

while I unscrew the nuts," he said, handing me a steel torch.

What a place for the car to break down, I wondered, looking furtively at the dark grove on both sides of the road. It was pitch dark and silent except for the occasional firefly and croaking of a frog. Uncle Siva had in the meantime unscrewed the defective wheel and was fitting the spare wheel while I was focusing the yellow circle of light from the torch to the hub of the wheel.

The story of the phantom boatman, the dark night, and the car breakdown in the middle of nowhere was actually not doing my constitution any good. I just wanted to get out of there and reach Madras. I realized I wasn't that brave after all.

"Damn!" swore Uncle Siva sweating profusely and trying to align the spare wheel with the nuts on the wheel hub. I could see his sinewy arms glisten in the dim light of the flashlight. Suddenly we could hear a creaking sound, barely audible yet clear and rhythmical; and it seemed to be steadily coming closer. It was getting closer. With shaking hands, I swung the flash light in the direction of the sound. Uncle Siva too squinted in the direction trying to figure out who or what it was. A figure of what appeared to be a man riding a cycle is what appeared to be approaching us.

The figure on the bicycle halted about 10 yards away from us. Even in the dim light of the torch we could make out that the man riding the bicycle was rather too big even for a grown-up human being. The huge man wore an ancient-looking crinkled shirt and loose pants in khaki colour, which seemed like some kind of uniform. His face was covered by a tattered hat and from what remained visible, we couldn't help but notice his thick beard underneath.

Before the two of us could say anything, the man said in a rather hoarse voice, "What are you doing here? Don't you know this is my beat area?"

Naturally, both of us were a little appalled by his bulk as well as peculiar turn out and gruff voice. However, Uncle

Siva said, "Sir, as you can see, we had a flat and I am almost done fixing it. We will be on our way soon."

"But you did not take my permission before stopping here. Where are my two rupees?" insisted the strange man coming closer. He smelled horrible, like putrefying garbage to say the least.

Uncle Siva was pretty irritated by now, convinced that the man was a good for nothing tramp who had lost his mental balance.

"What two rupees? You must be nuts. Get going! I am as it is tired and have been driving for a while…do not bother us anymore!"

Suddenly the weird man laughed…a most eerie and spine-chilling laugh, more like a wheeze. Uncle Siva was now angry and picking up the jack wrench after tightening the last nut and lowering the jack. He stood up and said in a menacing tone.

"You don't seem to understand decent language. Just move on. We to have got to go!" he said, motioning me to get into the car.

The weird man got back on his cycle and cycled off ahead of us in the darkness mumbling, "A debt is a debt. You will have to pay me."

I got back to my seat and closed the door while Uncle Siva went to put the tools and the punctured tyre in the boot. It must have been a minute or so.

Suddenly the weird man came next to the window of the car put his hand through and grabbed my shoulder and said, "You didn't take my permission… No one stops here without my permission and your uncle has not given me the two rupees which he owes me."

I was aghast with horror, and no words would come out of my throat – where the hell was Uncle Siva!?

My terror frozen mind could not comprehend much now.

"Muthu, Muthu what is wrong with you…" I sub

consciously heard a voice and felt someone shake my shoulder.

It was uncle Siva looking worried. "You seem to have dozed off and had a bad dream. That silly tramp must have scared you. We are done now and let's get going," said Uncle Siva turning the ignition of the car.

The car sputtered to life and he turned on the headlights. Back on the highway Uncle Siva accelerated the car. We reached a bridge on a river and crossed it. Suddenly in the headlights we saw the macabre cyclist standing in the middle of the road staring at us.

"What the…!" exclaimed Uncle Siva stamping on the brake pedal. The car squealed to a halt with a jerk.

The cyclist turned around and moved away from us mounting his ancient cycle. I let out a scream and pointed at the figure with a shivering finger. The man had no clothing on his back; his back was a sickening sight of rotting flesh with exposed bones that stretched till the waist line. Strange, slimy fluid oozed from the crevasses between the flesh and bones. The man slowly vanished into the darkness beyond. I do not recall what happened thereafter that night.

The next morning, a police patrol party found our car with its left wheels in a ditch beside the highway but with not much damage. It was a very accident-prone stretch immediately after the old bridge on the highway on the Then-Pennai River and was dotted with a few memorials of people who lost their lives at that place known locally as Robert's Bend after Head Constable Robert who lost his life at that very location way back in 1921 when there was no bridge there on the river. The bridge had come up about 20 years ago. Before that there was a causeway which used to get flooded in rainy season and the river had to be crossed on ferries. Legend states that he had drowned while trying to row a boat across the river to attend a distress call on a rainy night. His body had been found the next day badly mauled by the crocodiles in the river, with his back almost completely ripped off. He had been buried somewhere in the grove adjacent to the road.

I got away with minor scratches but poor Uncle Siva did not make it. Post mortem ruled that he had a massive cardiac arrest while driving and lost control of the car.

PS: The highway has since been re-aligned and is a six-lane highway now. Robert's Bend does not exist anymore and Uncle Siva is long gone. But I still do not believe that a sudden heart attack while on the wheel killed my Uncle that night, who was hale and hearty and all of 35 when he died. I can still swear that I had seen a grimace of terror, fright and shock on his face, when I saw his body for the first time that morning after I regained consciousness. I also never told anybody that when I checked the car's ash tray out of a morbid impulse that morning, there were only 9 Rupees change in all, in it.

Story **SEVEN**

THE TRISHUL KILLER CASE

The person who has devoured time is known as a Kapalik, one who calls home the skull of the sky, one who is the maker of the entire cosmos.
-Unknown

A train hooted and rumbled over tracks somewhere close by. A pesky mosquito was irritating Xavier no end, buzzing at his ear drums. The stake-out was getting boring and tiring. It was not like before any more. He remembered the times, almost 28 years back, when as a young inspector with the Bombay police, these kind of night stake-outs were almost routine and in fact used to cause a tinge of excitement, almost like the anticipation of watching a new crime thriller movie.

A lot of time had passed since then. He had been through

the thick and thin of gang wars in Bombay, seen the city become Mumbai and all the major gangsters either deceased or displaced. With the CBI now for 4 years, last two of which were spent in Delhi, life had generally been quiet barring routine investigations of corrupt low-ranking politicos. He had somehow steered clear of all the high-profile cases so far and with only 3 months to go for retirement, he was actually looking forward to settling down quietly at his village near Colva, Goa.

But like a ghost from a distant past, the "Trishul[43] Killer" seemed to be haunting him at the fag end of his innings. The Trishul Killer was the infamous serial killer who had kidnapped over 25 street children from South Bombay in the late 1980s and brutally killed them with a trident – supposedly for some hideous *tantric* child sacrifice ritual. Posted in the Crime Branch as a Sub-Inspector at that time he was assigned the job of investigating the case. After 1 ½ years of painstaking investigation he was finally able to crack the case and an *Aghori*[44] Tantric (an ascetic sadhu known to engage in post mortem black magic rituals in cremation grounds) named Rameshwar Baba had finally been nabbed. Investigations into the case though took a very severe physical, mental and emotional toll on Xavier. As one gory detail after other of the case started rolling out; including cannibalism, necrophilia and ruthless ritual dismemberment of small children, Xavier took heavily to drinking and smoking trying to forget the unbelievable depravity of the case. When the *Aghori* was finally caught red handed trying to lift another child at Sion, and brought up for investigation, Xavier and other policemen involved almost broke down themselves and had to control a very strong urge to strangle the hideous creature with their own hands when the tantric described one decadent deed after the other,

[43]Trident

[44]Refer trivia section for more details on "Aghoris"

almost nonchalantly. Sending him to the gallows was not very difficult with all the evidence piled up – It was a simple open and shut case. But Xavier took up the case personally in great detail to ensure there were no loose ends left.

The *Aghori's* demeanour throughout the investigation was unnerving and eerie to say the least. He would switch over to gibberish in some ancient language all of a sudden and start twitching and jerking. At other times he would glare at Xavier and the others with blazing eyes.

"The maniac must be having withdrawal symptoms without his daily dose of *Ganja*," Xavier would think. He knew that *Aghoris* and *tantrics* were habitual drug users – mostly of *Ganja* or Cannabis.

Finally, the Trial Court sentenced him to death after almost 1 year of hearings. The *Aghori* never represented to the higher courts – not because there was no one there to do it for him, but he simply did not seem interested in doing so himself.

As the day for his execution at Yerawada Jail in Pune dawned, Xavier made it a point to be present there to watch the beast swing from the hangman's rope. What happened on that day, suddenly came back to him in a flash in great detail at this moment. As the *Aghori* was being led off on his final walk to the gallows – he suddenly stopped on seeing Xavier – glared at him through bloodshot eyes and screamed in a guttural Hindi barring his yellow fangs, "An *Aghori* can never die! I will be back – don't forget all of you too are *Aghoris* deep inside…! And you infidel… You disturbed my penance, I will return and you will pay," he screamed pointing to Xavier.

The *Aghori's* words had disturbed him but he brushed it aside.

The case had definitely scarred him psychologically. It was two long years thereafter – two stints at the alcohol de-addiction centre and a near breakup of his marriage – that he finally managed to somewhat get it out of his system. He however, kept six unused iron tridents seized from the *Aghori* as morbid yet proud souvenirs of the landmark case. Probably he could show them off to his grandchildren someday, he thought.

When kidnapping and murders of two small children in quick succession were reported in South Delhi in a month's time and the murder weapon was a 'Trishul' in both cases, it seemed too uncannily similar to the happenings in Bombay 28 years ago; *too similar for coincidence*! The department had naturally assigned him the case when they found out that he had been the investigating officer the last time over.

"It definitely cannot be the same guy… I saw him hang in front of my eyes and then cremated at the prison itself. This seems to be some tantric ritual – being done by another *Aghori*," wondered Xavier. During his investigation the last time, he had done a lot of reading up and research on tantric practices and rituals, which had actually helped him reach the murderer successfully and catch him red handed.

This time however, Xavier neither had the energy nor the appetite to investigate and crack the case. He was honestly looking forward to his retirement and cursed the murderer under his breath for not starting his vile deeds some 3 months hence, so that he could have spent his residual few days as a policeman quietly. But now he was burdened with the case, given a desk with a phone in the Vasant Vihar Police Station and given a rookie cop as his assistant.

"Do they really expect me to crack this case…?" he wondered pessimistically.

Xavier looked at his young partner, ASI[45] Yaduveer Yadav, a 25-year-old lad with clear features, new to the force, all enthusiastic and eager to learn. Xavier couldn't control a smile when he saw the young man drool as he dozed over the

---

[45]Assistant Sub Inspector

dashboard of the unmarked Indica car in which they were keeping a vigil near Munirka Village. Having a sudden urge to relieve himself, Xavier got down from the car and walked to a dark corner of the alleyway. After the job was done, he zipped up his fly and started moving back to the car. There was not a single soul to be seen anywhere around. Suddenly, from the corner of his eye he spotted a movement towards his left, and saw a shadow slip through the edge of the nearest building through the wintry smog. Instinctively, he tiptoed behind it, feeling the reassuring bulge of his service revolver in his shoulder holster, hidden below his woollen jacket.

"Is it an animal…or is it a beggar?" he wondered as he saw a bedraggled form at a distance. Suddenly, he tripped and fell down with a thud.

He got up disoriented and tried to recall what had happened. "Hell! I must have passed out for a while," he muttered angrily as he checked his watch which showed the time as 3:35 a.m. He clearly remembered that it was around 1 a.m. when he had got down from the vehicle for a leak. His legs and arms were stiff from the cold and his body was aching. He saw that the spot he had fallen down was at the end of the road, about 150 yards from where the car stood. Having been reasonably assured that there was no major damage done, he gingerly limped back to the car. He sat on his seat and thereafter could not resist dozing off as by now, Yaduveer was in deep slumber and was snoring loudly.

"Sirji, sirji…get up!"

Xavier got up with a start when he found Yaduveer frantically tugging at his shoulders.

"What happened? What time is it…?" said Xavier groggily. "Sir, it is 6:30 a.m., …and real bad news to start the day!" said Yaduveer.

Xavier was startled to see two police cars standing at the other end of the road and an ambulance pull up down the road.

"Sir! the bastard has struck again…under our very

noses," said Yaduveer full of indignation, almost as though his manhood had taken a beating. "A child has been done to death in the next block!"

Both of them went near the spot where the patrol car stood, about 140-150 yards from their location. Recognizing him, the driver saluted and pointed down the lane which led to the neighbouring block. They knew they had reached near the crime scene as the wailing and lamenting of women from a nearby hut was now audible. It was the hut which housed the family of a *press-wallah*[46] , who eked out a modest living by pressing clothes of the residents of the colony. Xavier found the heavy coal charged iron box lying outside the hut.

As per the SI on the site, it emerged that the *press-wallah* had had one drink too many last night and had passed out in a drunken stupor. His wife had put their 5-year-old daughter to sleep and then herself slept off. It was late at night, way past midnight (she did not remember the exact time), that she was woken up by the sound of the flimsy door of their hut closing. To her horror she found her child missing from her side. She immediately ran out and saw a figure carrying her child move out into the darkness. Apparently, she ran screaming after the figure and tried to snatch her child back, when she was hit on her face by a blunt object and then she had lost conscious.

Early in the morning, an elderly morning walker's dog had traced blood stains on the road that led him to a thicket about a kilometre away. The horrified senior citizen found the child's body lying in an appalling condition and he promptly called the cops.

"Sir, they found an iron trishul embedded in the chest of the child," said Yaduveer dryly.

Xavier, suddenly remembered the shadowy figure he had tracked last night. Was it related in some way to this, he

---

[46]Person who irons clothes for a living

wondered.

"I must meet the child's mother," he told the SI as they moved into the hut. A frail, dark woman was wailing inconsolably at one corner of the hut and a few other women were lamenting along with her. The *press wallah*, clearly an advanced alcoholic with a gaunt, hunched frame was in a daze. Realizing that both were in no condition to answer any questions right now, Xavier and Yaduveer turned to leave. Suddenly, the child's mother glanced towards them and with a loud shriek, swooned.

"Poor thing! The child must have been her only happiness in life. That too is gone. Must have been too much for her. Please give her some sedative and move her to the hospital," said Xavier to the paramedic who had come with the ambulance waiting outside.

Back at the Station after freshening up, Xavier realized that some of his zeal to trap the murderer had surprisingly come back. Probably the grisly murder of the child had once again played upon his conscience.

"We must first draw a pattern…and then zero down on the suspects," said Xavier to Yaduveer as he began plotting the Trishul Killer's trail for a second time in his life, albeit after 28 years.

The first killing had been on 7th November 2014 in Basant Gaon, the urban village near Vasant Vihar, of a presumably orphaned female street child aged about 10 years, not identified yet. The child had been done to death by the 'trishul' and then decapitated. Without the head, the child could not be identified. It might have just passed over as an insignificant crime, but for the apparent ritualistic nature of the murder. Vermillion powder had been spread over the body and lemon and chilies tied over the crude iron trident which had been used to pierce the heart of the orphan.

The second murder had occurred, almost a month later in the cold of the night of 6th December 2014. This time, it was an 8-year-old male child of a low-ranking Government official who lived in the LIG[47] Flats in RK Puram. The child had gone to the park to play and had not come back until 8 p.m. The worried parents and sibling (a 12-year-old elder brother) frantically searched for the child, but in vain. The next day, the unfortunate child's body, intact this time, was found in a trash dump in nearby Moti Bagh. But this murder too seemed ritualistic, as the child had been tonsured, and its forehead marked with vermillion, before being done to death by an iron trident piercing its heart.

It was thereafter, that the case had been assigned to Xavier.

"Both murders in South Delhi and now this third one too", wondered Xavier. It is almost as though the dead Aghori psychopath from his distant past was trying to test him again, considering that Xavier himself now used to live in South Delhi; Vasant Kunj to be precise.

"Sir, do you know what 7th November, 6th December and yesterday were!" said Yaduveer excitedly looking up from is laptop.

"No, what is special about these dates except that this bastard butchered those poor children on them?" said Xavier.

"They were all full moon nights," said Yaduveer in a nervous tone. "Sir, I don't like this one bit," he murmured.

"Just see when is the next full moon, he is sure to strike then," said Xavier.

"3rd February is the date," said Yaduveer, not looking up from his laptop screen.

Almost 25 days passed without event and the investigations in the Munirka murder also drew a big blank like the previous two cases. It was 31st January when the SI of Munirka Police Station called up on the land line to speak to Xavier. But Xavier had not yet come in and so Yaduveer took the call. The SI informed him that the *press wallah's* wife had

---

[47]Lower income group

given her statement a day earlier. Her statement was similar to what he had said when they had met on the day of the murder, except the fact that she had said something about again seeing the killer once more after that day. Only she could not clearly remember when or where, as she was not yet fully mentally stable. He was getting a sketch made of the killer from her description. The same would be ready in 3-4 days' time, after which he would share the same with them. Yaduveer thanked him for the input and put the phone down when Xavier walked in.

Yaduveer told him what had transpired in brief. "I hope she knows what she's saying and does not lead us off on a wild goose chase," said Xavier. "Anyways let's get ready properly for the next full moon night, this time we must not let him slip. Tell him to hurry up with the sketch, so that we can have it before the 3rd."

All policemen on beat all over Delhi had been asked to be extra vigilant on 3rd February 2015. A TV bulletin and newspaper release by the police warned all parents to be more careful about the safety of their children.

3rd February dawned but the sketch was not yet ready. The SI promised to send it across by evening.

"Let's move out at around 6 p.m. Can you pick me up from my place?" said Xavier to Yaduveer, picking up his bag and heading home to freshen up, around 4 p.m.

At 5:45 p.m., Yaduveer was at Xavier's place at Vasant Kunj. He rang the doorbell and heard Xavier's voice asking him to come in as the door was not locked. He saw Xavier poring over a map with a tantric symbol in his other hand looking very excited.

"I think I got a pattern, just like the last time!" said Xavier, pointing out at a few crosses marked on the map. "I superimposed this *yantra*[48], on the map, and also marked

---

[48]Religious or occult symbol

the lats and longs of the last three crime sites. I think I have zeroed down upon the exact location where he is going to strike tonight!"

An encircled red cross was marked in the general area of the ancient Sultan Garhi monument located towards the Northern end of Vasant Kunj, not very far from where they were located.

Visibly impressed, Yaduveer asked him, "That is very precise Sir, but how can you be so sure?" "I studied tantric symbology and practices the last time over and it helped me nab the Mumbai Trishul Killer. All these ritual killings follow a pattern and certain conventions; hopefully I should have got it right this time too."

"Sir, we must surround the place and arrange for at least 3 to 4 PCRs…let me call up the SHO" said Yaduveer excitedly.

"No! We both go alone… I want to trap the bastard. He's very smart. Too much of fanfare will drive him away. He will need his pound of flesh tonight, he will end up killing somewhere else and we might lose him till the next full moon!"

Checking their fire arms, the duo left. Xavier as usual carried his duffel bag. Yaduveer smiled and remembered their previous stake-out – Xavier always carried his regulation hip flask filled with Old Monk Rum and chicken sandwiches in the bag, both of which he had to politely refuse for he was a teetotaller and a vegetarian.

They were there close to the Sultan Garhi monument – an ancient mausoleum from the pre-Mughal era. An area formerly notorious for drug peddlers, prostitutes and eunuchs to ply their trade after sunset. However, a public outcry by residents of Vasant Kunj a few years ago, had resulted in a clean-up operation police and the area was generally quiet and crime free since then. As it was nearing 9:00 p.m., the few evening walkers and pedestrians had thinned out and the place was almost deserted now. The radio in the unmarked

Tata Indica played Radio Mirchi with the RJ chattering away nonstop about the traffic snarl at Mulchand Flyover and the bad quality of air in Delhi.

"Why can't they play some music for a change?" said Xavier in an irritated tone.

He rummaged inside his bag which seemed to contain a plethora of stuff, pulled out his hip flask and took a swig of Old Monk rum.

The night passed on eventless. Yaduveer, scared that he would doze off like the last time, suggested that they could take a walk around to spot anything unusual.

"No! We will just wait quietly here, the view will be perfect in the full moon, which will rise soon. I don't want us to be doing anything to scare him away from here," said Xavier in hushed tones. "I knew you'll feel sleepy, I have got some coffee for you!" he added with a wink and dished out a small thermos flask from his all-encompassing bag. He poured some coffee for Yaduveer in the lid and handed it out.

"Thank you, Sir! As a matter of fact, I was feeling sleepy!" said Yaduveer, gratefully accepting the drink. He slowly sipped the coffee. It was a little too bitter for his liking but he politely continued to sip the beverage.

The coffee, instead of waking him up seemed to make him drowsier and he began dozing as the bracing February breeze wafted through the open window of the car. Xavier too seemed to be cat-napping besides him.

Yaduveer got up with a start and checked his mobile phone. The time was 1:30 am and the moonlight was bright and illuminated the old monument in front of him clearly. Xavier was not there besides him.

"Shit! Sir must have got a trace of something. He should have woken me up and taken me along," wondered Yaduveer, almost guiltily.

In spite of his extreme drowsiness, he got out of the car and went silently towards the monument. A WhatsApp message came on his phone followed by three missed calls, which he did not realize, as he had put his phone on silent mode and tucked it into his jacket pocket before getting down from the car.

He had walked about 200 yards and reached the winding steep stairs made of stone, and supported by pillars and flooring which led to the *Ghari* (cave) which held the crypt or the tomb. The cave was covered by an unusual octagonal roof slab. It was pitch dark inside, and Yaduveer had to resist the temptation of switching on his torch. As he neared the cave, he suddenly stopped. He thought that he had heard something inside the cave. His blood almost froze when he heard a low but distinct crackling voice from inside the cave. He gripped his pistol for re-assurance and decided to go closer.

"No one can break my penance…no one…not even you, you infidel! You disturbed it many years ago, but I told you I will be back!" he heard a guttural voice in Hindi followed by a shrill eerie laughter.

Before he could react, he heard Xavier's distinct voice, "You are dead, I saw you die…I will kill you again this time with my bare hands. Leave this child *now*!"

Yaduveer decided it was time to intervene. He pulled out his pistol and switching on his flash light jumped into the cave. He froze in horror when he found no one except Xavier standing there.

It was indeed Xavier, with vermillion powder smeared on his forehead and ash smeared on his face and holding an iron trident in his hand. He swung the light of the torch on the dark shadow on the ground and found the prone form of a thin child, a rag picker by the looks of it – dead with an iron trident embedded in its chest.

"*You are again trying to disturb my penance*!!!" screamed Xavier in a guttural Hindi in a shrill surreal voice.

Shocked, disoriented and still drowsy from the strange tasting coffee, which he was now sure, had been laced by

Xavier, he brought up his pistol and pulled the trigger. There was an ineffectual click as the hammer struck the empty chamber. He put his finger under the butt and was horrified to find that there was no magazine.

With a loud yell, Xavier jumped on Yaduveer, hit him on the head with a blunt object and stabbed him thrice in quick succession in the chest with the iron trident with surprisingly brute force. Mortally wounded, Yaduveer lay gasping.

Xavier came up to him again and Yaduveer winced for another assault.

Suddenly, Xavier said, "Yaduveer, what happened to you…? Who did this to you?" His voice was normal.

Yaduveer could not understand what was happening.

Suddenly, Xavier's voice changed to the same guttural tone and he screamed, "*I am an Aghori…I am beyond life and death…! Nobody disturbs my penance…!*".

With these words he pulled out a *khukri* from his duffel bag and stabbed Yaduveer's already limp body in the stomach till he was dead. The cave was filled with shrill hysterical laughter. The duffel bag had spilt its contents on the floor, which also contained an unused iron trident, identical to the two others used for stabbing the child and Yaduveer. It was an ordinary crude trident and was etched with the manufacturer's mark and year of manufacture "Laxmi Iron Works, Bombay, 1986".

Yaduveer's mobile fell out of his pocket and lay on the floor. It still had the unread WhatsApp message. It was from the SI of Vasant Vihar and so had been the three missed calls. The message had the sketch made by the police artist from the description given by the *press wallah's* wife.

The sketch quite resembled Xavier.

Story **EIGHT**

VACATION IN McCLUSKIEGUNGE

A walk in nature, walks the soul back home.
– Mary Davis

Bhaskar was lost, hot, tired, and angry. As he dawdled his way through the arid featureless field that looked very similar to the last one, in grim landscape stretching up to the horizon, he cursed the tiny settlement of McCluskiegunge,[49] the old hag – his grandmother – for living in it, and above all, his mother for dragging him from their comfortable house in Calcutta and dumping him there. When he got back to grandma's house he would give it to the two women and tell them how much he hated being here. But right now, he was hopelessly

[49]Refer trivia section for more details on McCluskiegunge.

lost; and his priority was to locate the goddamned house.

He stopped and looked around yet again to spot something familiar. An elevated ground would have afforded him a view of the area around, and from where he could spot his grandmother's crumbling old house. Strangely, in spite of McCluskiegunge being located in rolling country, the place where he was walking now, was perfectly flat.

Bhaskar was seventeen years old, tall, muscular and quite good looking. He had inherited blue eyes and a muscular build from his quarter European blood. Right now, he was completely peeved. If anyone back from his School – South Point School in Calcutta – had seen him stumbling around an empty field in the middle of nowhere, they'd have laughed at him.

It was another matter that nobody dared to laugh at Bhaskar Ghosh for he was the quintessential class bully: not at his name, not at his place in class (always last), not at anything about him. Generally, people avoided him, which suited Bhaskar fine. He loved being the bully, tormenting other children and seeing the fear loom in their eyes.

He was dragging his feet wearily, quite exhausted physically and mentally, when Bhaskar's foot struck a burrow pit in the ground and he fell on his face with his hands outstretched. He managed to save himself from falling, but a bolt of pain shot up his leg as his ankle twisted. He swore loudly, the four-letter word that always made his mother wince nervously. She had given up trying to talk him out of using bad language. He was taller than her now and he very well knew that subconsciously even she was scared of him. Sometimes, she would meekly try to advise him; but eventually her words would fall on deaf ears.

He brushed the dust and got up grimacing in agony, and looked at the burrow pit which had caused the fall. It was no ordinary burrow pit. It seemed to be an old earthen grave which had been dug up by a jackal or some other wild animal. He shuddered as he saw something which looked like a human bone sticking out of the hole. He observed that there were a few such earthen graves around on that field, probably an old *Adivasi*[50] graveyard. He shivered in spite of the heat and all the more wanted to get away from that place and get back home.

Bhaskar was Margaret Ghosh's only child. Her husband – Sanjoy Ghosh – had been an accountant at the State Bank. One day while at work he just collapsed and never got up again. They said it was a massive cardiac arrest. Bhaskar could never get along with his father and hadn't really missed him – particularly when he realized that he was now the man of the house.

Mother and Son lived in a two-room apartment in the crowded Ultadanga area of Calcutta. There were two small insurance policies and the bank provided a modest pension, hence Margaret Ghosh was able to keep it after Sanjoy's passing. Even then, she'd had to go back to work to support Bhaskar and herself…no need to ask which of the two was the more expensive.

Fancy vacations to Darjeeling were out of the question. As much as Bhaskar whined and complained, Margaret couldn't find the money. But her mother, Rosalyn Thipthorpe lived on a farm in the old Anglo-Indian settlement of McCluskiegunge in Bihar (now Jharkhand); and once or twice a year, in the summer and during the Pooja break, the two of them made the 10-hour train journey up from Calcutta to McCluskiegunge, and onwards to '*Rosemary*' the old stone house just outside the settlement, where the old lady had been living for years. Margaret's father Joseph Thipthorpe had been a plate-layer with the Bengal Nagpur Railway (BNR) and he and her mother were one of the original settlers of McCluskiegunge. Rosalyn continued to live there even after Joseph passed away

---

[49]Tribal

about a decade ago.

McCluskiegunge was a very quaint old town, where time seemed to have stood still. A pathway ran up from the main road, past a line of Ashoka[51] trees and a smattering of old houses – mostly unoccupied – since most of the Anglos had migrated out of the place in the 60s and 70s. A single horse *tonga* was transporting both of them from the railway station and the horse cart was bumping uncomfortably on the un-metalled pathway.

"Isn't it beautiful?" said Margaret, while the tonga was moving in the tree lined rutted path.

A couple of black crows swooped overhead and landed in a nearby field. At the end of the track a rickety iron gate with a rusty sign board proclaimed '*Rosemary*' indicating that they had reached their destination.

Bhaskar read aloud the signboard with no enthusiasm. His mother had sighed. "I was so happy here once."

But where was it? Where the hell was Rosemary NOW?

As he crossed what he now realized was a quite enormous field, Bhaskar found himself wincing with every step. He was also beginning to feel the first stirrings of…something, a primordial fear; and he was very angry too. But he was beginning to wonder just how much farther he would have to walk before he knew where he was; and in his present condition he didn't know how much more he could actually walk.

Bhaskar had allowed his mother to talk him into coming, knowing that if he complained hard enough she would be forced to bribe him with a handful of audio cassettes at the very least. Sure enough, he had passed the journey from Calcutta to McCluskiegunge listening to the latest Disco Hits on his Walkman and had been in a good enough mood to give his grandmother a quick peck on the cheek when they

---

[51] *Saraca asoca*, a common tree native to India

arrived.

"You've grown so much," the old lady had exclaimed as he slouched into a battered armchair in the living room. "Maggie – you look so pale…you have not been taking care of yourself!" she continued.

Bhaskar noisily yawned at the cliched lines Granny repeated every time they visited.

"Mum, I'm okay – don't worry," said Margaret.

"You don't look well. But the air of McCluskie will clear you out."

A week here in this godforsaken hell-hole!

As he limped onward and onward through the field, swatting at a wretched fly that was circling his head, Bhaskar thought longingly of concrete roads, bus stops, traffic lights, and eating his favourite street food. At last, he reached the hedge that divided this field from the next and he grabbed at it, tearing at the leaves with his bare hands. Too late, he saw the nettle like leaves commonly known as *bichua jhari* behind the hedge. Bhaskar yelped, bringing his clenched hand to his lips. A string of white bumps rose up, scattered across the palm and the insides of his fingers.

What was so great about the countryside? His crazy Anglo-Indian grandmother went on rambling about the peace, the fresh air, all the usual rubbish spouted by people who wouldn't even recognize a traffic light if they saw one. People with no life, no ambition at all.

"The flowers, the trees, the birds and the meandering streams. Everything is different in McCluskie," she would say. "You are at peace. You don't feel time rushing past you. You can stand out here and imagine how things were before people spoiled everything with their noise and their machines. You can still feel the magic in the countryside. The power of Mother Nature. It's all around you. Alive. Waiting…"

Bhaskar had listened to the old woman and sneered. She was obviously getting senile. There was no magic in the countryside, only days that seemed to drag on forever and nights with nothing to do. She did not even have a TV. This was the year 1995; and Mother Nature, even if the old girl had existed, which was unlikely, had been finished off by the cities long ago, buried under miles of roads, concrete monstrosities and mounds of garbage. For Bhaskar, travelling on the highway with music in full blast, or loafing around with his friends was magic – and not this!

After a few days of lazing around the house, Bhaskar had allowed his grandmother to persuade him to go for a walk. The truth was that he was bored by the two women, and, anyway, out in the fields he would be able to smoke a couple of the cigarettes he had bought with money stolen from his mother's handbag.

"Make sure you follow the footpaths, Bhaskar," his mother had said.

"And don't forget the countryside's code of conduct," his grandmother had added.

Bhaskar remembered the countryside code of conduct all right. As he ambled away from *Rosemary*, he picked wildflowers and tore them to shreds. When he came to a gate he deliberately left it open, smiling to himself as he thought of the farm animals that might now wander onto the road.

He drank a Coke and flung the empty plastic bottle into the middle of a meadow full of buttercups. He half snapped the branch off an apple tree and left it dangling there. He smoked a cigarette and threw the butt, still glowing, into the long grass and he made it a point to stay off the footpath.

Perhaps that hadn't been such a good idea. He was lost before he knew it. He was tramping through a field, crushing the crop underfoot, when he realized that the ground was getting soft and mushy. His foot broke through the corn or whatever it was and water curled over his shoe, soaking into his sock. Bhaskar grimaced, thought for a moment, and decided to go back the way he had come…

Only the way he had come was somehow no longer there. It should have been. He had left enough landmarks, after all. But suddenly the broken branch, the Coke bottle, and the torn-up plants had vanished. Nor was there any sign of the footpath. In fact, there was nothing at all that Bhaskar recognized. It was rather strange. That had been over two hours ago. Moreover, there was not a single soul in sight nor any sign of human habitation.

Since then, things had gone from bad to worse. Bhaskar had made his way through a small thicket and had managed to scratch his shoulder and gash his leg on the wicked brambles of a *kikar*[52] bush.

A moment later he had backed into a tree that had torn his favourite jacket, a navy-blue zip up jacket that he had shoplifted from the big cloth shop in Burra Bazar.

He had managed to get out of the thicket – but even that hadn't been easy. Suddenly he had found a small stream in his path (surprisingly he had not crossed it on his way out) and the only way to cross it had been to balance on a log that was lying in the middle. He had almost done it, too, but at the last minute the log had rolled from under his foot, hurling him backward into the water. He had stood up spluttering and swearing. Ten minutes later he had stopped to have another cigarette, but the whole pack was drenched and destroyed.

And now…

Now he screamed as the insect, which he had assumed was a fly but in fact was a wasp, which stung him on the side of the neck. He pulled at his damp and dirty grey T-shirt, squinting down to see the damage. Out of the corner of his eye he could just make out the edge of a huge, red swelling. He shifted his weight onto his bad foot and groaned as fresh pain shuddered upward. Where the heck was *Rosemary*?

This was all his mother's fault. And his grandmother's.

[52]Indian gum arabic plant

They were the ones who'd suggested the walk. Well, they'd pay for it. Perhaps they'd think twice about how lovely the countryside was when they saw their precious house go up in smoke – and he meant it. He practically wanted to burn down the house so that he would never have to visit the wretched place ever again.

And then he saw it. The grey walls and slanting tiled roof were unmistakable.

Somehow, he had found his way back. He had only one more field to cross and he'd be there. There was a path of sorts going around the side of the field, but he wasn't having any of that. He walked straight across the middle. It had been freshly sown. Too bad!

This field was even bigger than the one he had just crossed and the sun seemed to be hotter than ever. The soil was soft and his feet sank into it. His ankle was on fire, and every step he took, his legs seemed to get heavier and heavier. The wasp wouldn't leave him alone either. It was buzzing around his head, round and round, the noise drilling into his skull. But Bhaskar was too tired to swat at it again. His tired arms hung lifelessly in their sockets, his fingertips brushing against the legs of his jeans. The smell of the freshly ploughed earth filled his nostrils, rich and deep. The smell of moist cow dung manure and petrichor was making him feel sick.

He had walked now for fifteen minutes, maybe longer. But *Rosemary* was no closer. It was now blurred, shimmering on the edge of his vision. He wondered if he was suffering from sunstroke. Surely it hadn't been as hot as this when he set out?

Every step was becoming more difficult. It was as if his feet were trying to root themselves in the ground. He looked back (whimpering as his collar rubbed the wasp sting) and saw with relief that he was exactly halfway across the field. Rivulets of sweat poured from his head and dripped off his chin.

He couldn't go any farther. There was a pole stuck in the ground ahead of him and Bhaskar seized hold of it gratefully. He would have to rest for a while. The ground was too soft and damp to sit on, so he would rest standing up, holding on to the pole. Just a few minutes. Then he would cross the rest of the field.

When the sun began to set and there was still no sign of Bhaskar, his grandmother called the police. The local police inspector took a description of the lost boy and that same night they began a cross-country search that would go on for the next seven days. But there was no trace of him.

The police thought he might have stepped into a car with a stranger, or he might have been kidnapped. But nobody had seen anything nor were there any calls for ransom. All hospitals and police stations up to Ranchi, Jamshedpur and Patna had drawn a blank. It was as if the countryside had taken him and swallowed him up, as one policeman said.

Bhaskar watched as the policc finally left. He watched as his mother carried her suitcase out of *Rosemary* and got into the *tonga* that would take her back to McCluskiegunge station and her train to Calcutta. He was glad to see that she had the decency to cry, mourning her loss. But he couldn't help feeling that she looked rather less tired and rather less ill than she had when she arrived.

Margaret did not see him. As she waved goodbye to her mother and *Rosemary*, she did notice that this time there were no crows in the nearby field. She quickly realized why. They had been scared away by a figure that was standing in the middle of a nearby field, propped up on a dried bamboo stick. For a moment she thought she recognized its torn navy-blue jacket and the grimy T-shirt. But she was probably confused and tired...and was she really interested? The *tonga* bounced past the new scarecrow and continued down past the waving Ashoka trees to the main road.

Story **NINE**

THE BATTLE OF HENKAR

In one aspect, yes, I believe in ghosts, but we create them. We haunt ourselves.
-Laurie Halse Anderson

The air was cold and dry…so dry that the insides of the nostrils felt sore. At the elevation of 14,000 feet, oxygen was scanty. This, coupled with the darkness of the night, the silhouettes of the treeless hilltops around, and the steady rattling of the tin sheet roofs of the shelters in the wind only made the night more surreal and eerie. The Henkar Post lay bang short of the Shoka La Pass which marked the border between India and China. The post guarded one of the most important approaches from the pass into the Siang Valley, which further led to major towns and settlements southwards. It was due to its strategic location that Henkar had been the scene of a major battle[53] during the infamous Sino-Indian Military Conflict of 1962.

On the fateful night of 24 October, 1962, about 500 Chinese soldiers attacked Henkar. Though greatly outnumbered, with a mere strength of about 50 troops, the Indian troops fought back tenaciously. Though the Assam Rifles platoon holding the post inflicted heavy casualties on the Chinese, ultimately, after fierce fighting, including hand-to-hand combat, the greatly outnumbered Indian troops were forced to withdraw. Today was incidentally 24th October 2012 – but exactly 50 years after the battle.

Remote military posts in the mountains, especially those with bloody or tragic pasts, invariably had their local legends of hauntings, resident ghosts (both of the benevolent and malevolent varieties) and supposedly paranormal activity. Most of these were just figments of imagination of superstitious and lonely soldiers mostly from simple rural backgrounds.

Henkar was no exception. The legend of ghostly Chinese soldiers appearing on every 24th October was its own pet legend and lots of the old timers actually claim witnessing this phenomenon first hand. I heard about it first from Dal Bahadur.

Havildar[54] Dal Bahadur Lohar who was the old NCO who accompanied me all the way up from the road head, Tato, a good 5-day, 72 km trek along the treacherous mountain trails, had kept me regaled with folklore of the area, all through the 5 arduous days. For a man who had not seen the world beyond Along, the District Headquarters, he was surprisingly knowledgeable. His father had been a military porter during the '62 war and Dal himself recalled seeing Chinese soldiers marching through the valley right up to Tato. It was during

---

[53]Refer trivia section for more details on the actual battle.

[54]Sergeant in Indian Army.

one of our night halts enroute in a village headman's house, after being duly fortified with three stiff shots of rum, that Dal Bahadur first told me about the Battle of Henkar and that bloody night when the Chinese were contested fiercely and practically halted for the whole night – giving sufficient time for moving heavy artillery pieces to defend important locations in the depth. He did mention the folklore about ghost Chinese soldiers being seen around Henkar especially around the anniversary of the battle each year. He however, said that he had personally never witnessed such a thing, but had heard it from a few who had done so. I laughed it off.

I stood at the sentry post located on a vantage point facing North and peered from the infra-red binoculars into the darkness. I could clearly make out the narrow path leading down from the pass down to the post and beyond.

The duty guard who was a young Gorkha sepoy, finding me shivering in the cold (which I was still not really accustomed to) told me, "Sahib! I'll just go down to the post and fetch some hot tea for you!"

I smiled and nodded gratefully to him. The post was about 100 metres behind the sentry post and to my right somewhere, was the machine gun nest with the gun on fixed line covering the path I just mentioned.

I rubbed by palms and scanned the surroundings with the IR device again, and again viewed the path. Did I spot some movement there? I swallowed a lump in my throat and focused again. Nothing! My eyes must be playing tricks on me, I told myself and waited impatiently for the guard to return with hot tea.

I then heard a sound… Somewhat like a neighing of a horse form the direction of the pass. What the hell was that…? I instinctively focused the IR device in that direction. I almost swooned at what I could see. I could make out a number of human figure like outlines topped with a round shape, something similar to a military helmet, and yes I could see the shape of something which appeared to be a pack mule or a horse, and a couple of smaller shapes, presumably dogs. There were quite a few of the human figures coming down the path, less than a kilometre from the post. I yelled out to the machine gun crew about 100-150 odd metres to my right. However, I did not get any acknowledgement. I immediately called on my walkie talkie set, back to the post, but could hear only static.

Suddenly, I heard the staccato of a machine gun open up from just below the vantage point I stood on. I was a little surprised, since I thought the machine gun nest was a little farther away. But how did it matter – so long as the gunner had seen the apparent intrusion and opened up. Rat-a-tat! Rat-a-tat! The firing continued and I could see the path of the tracers leading straight to where I had seen the activity.

I looked at the path and found the red outlined human figures go into a tizzy and then saw them too opening up with small arms.

"These are no ghosts!" I exclaimed, as I saw the exchange of fire in progress.

However, since I heard no movement or sound coming from the side of the post, which was surprising, I decided to go back and alert and rally them. In any case I was only carrying a pistol which was of no use at this range.

The Chinese suddenly fired some kind of a flare which lit up the whole scenario. I instinctively shielded eyes and tried to figure out the exact location of our machine gun nest which was so effectively holding back the Chinks. Right below the guard post was the place from where the gun was firing. I saw the backs of two soldiers hunched over the gun; one was operating the gun and another guiding the ammo belt into it.

But wait! Why were these blokes in summer uniforms in this biting cold?

"Hang on guys! I am just alerting the post! We will nail these guys!" I yelled out to them. The gunner's helper looked up and waved. The flare went out that very moment.

What I saw, suddenly cut out the oxygen to my brain and I must have blacked out after that. The last thing I remembered was that the gunner's helper's face had no flesh but only a bleached skull as a façade and the hand which waved out to me was skeletal and the arm it was attached to, was wrapped in a tattered uniform.

Somebody was opening my eyes and shining a flashlight at it.

"Can you hear me Sahib?" I heard a familiar voice call out anxiously. I gingerly opened my eyes and found myself lying on the bed in the tiny sick quarters of Henkar Post. Dal Bahadur was looking at me with a very worried look on his face. The paramedic NCO was busy measuring my blood pressure.

"What happened to me?" I asked Dal Bahadur.

"We don't know Sahib! When Padma Bahadur (the young sentry who had gone to fetch tea for me) came back with the tea he found you shouting at someone from the guard post. Then he heard you crashing down on the floor all of a sudden," he replied.

"What happened to the Chinese?" I asked in a shrill voice.

"What Chinese Sahib?" replied Dal Bahadur.

"I saw so many of them coming down the path…didn't anyone hear any gunfire!?" I retorted.

The three-four people in the sick bay exchanged blank glances and shrugged. "Sir, there are no Chinese and no one came. There is no report of any such thing from any sentry. It will be dawn soon and we will check again. Pardon me, Sir, but dark nights in mountains do play a lot of tricks on the eyes and on the mind," said Dal Bahadur.

I must have slept off again as the paramedic had probably given me a sedative to calm my nerves and bring down my B.P. I woke up after a few hours definitely feeling calmer and felt the comforting rays of the sun gently falling on my face through the sky light. I walked out of the sick bay and found Dal Bahadur, Padma and a few other soldiers having an animated conversation over something in *Gorkhali*[55] , only I could make out it was about me as I heard the words 'Captain Sahib'. They snapped to attention the moment they saw me. But what was with them was a surprise. It was a beautiful golden coated Labrador with a leather collar.

"Never seen him before – where has he come from?" I asked Dal.

"Sir, we do not know…but you must see this," said Dal pointing to a metal tag attached to the collar. It was something written in Chinese but it had the unmistakable red star with a golden border – the insignia of the Chinese Army, the PLA. It was undoubtedly a PLA tracker dog which had somehow strayed to the post.

"Sir, we found him loitering around a few hours back near the garbage pit behind the post," said Padma.

"Sahib! Sahib!" suddenly I heard a voice call out from a distance. I turned towards the direction. I saw a soldier running towards the post.

"Sir, that is Purna the perimeter patrol leader. Wonder what he has to say?" said Dal Bahadur.

"Sir, you need to come with me. Need to show you something," said Purna.

We followed Purna as he took us down the small valley towards the North of the post and towards the path that led up to the pass. We walked for about a kilometre when he motioned us to halt. He had already deployed his scouts to be on the lookout. He nervously pointed at a rock adjacent to the path and also at the path ahead. The rock had a number of holes as though it had been hit with a burst of gunfire. On the path ahead lay a few random pieces of kit such as a broken helmet, a piece of a saddle, a boot and a water bottle

[53]A language spoken by Nepalese

– all of which were definitely not Indian Army issue, and all of them appeared to be of vintage designs. Also, there were quite few footprints on the overnight snow and some marks which looked like bloodstains.

I turned to Dal Bahadur and the others standing next to me who had shocked looks on their faces.

"I told you so…there had been Chinese here last night. This explains it and explains the lost dog as well. Our machine gunners did a good job and beat them back. Wonder how you guys did not hear it!" I admonished them.

Now I was sure that my eyes had indeed played tricks and I had actually imagined I saw that skeletal figure last night.

"Come… Let's go to the machine gun nest and get to the bottom of this. I will have to report this to the Brigade Headquarters thereafter," I said leading them back to the post.

As we trudged back to the post, I turned towards the guard post and the location where I had seen the machine gun nest last night. "Sir, the machine gun nest is in this direction," said Dal pointing towards the left.

"How's that possible? Dal you are disoriented I think," I said a tad irritated.

He and the others then quietly followed me.

We reached the guard post and I looked around for the machine gun nest. There was nothing to be seen except a white-washed stone marker with incense sticks lit near it. The soldiers exchanged nervous glances.

"Sir, did you say that the MG post was here?" asked Dal.

"Yes, I believe it was here that I saw it," I replied with a perplexed look on my face.

"Sir, this is the memorial of Naik[56] Ranjeet Thapa and Rifleman Ram Bahadur, and marks the spot where there used to be a machine gun bunker long ago. Ranjeet and Ram were the two machine gunners who held back the Chinese during

---

[56]Corporal in Indian Army

the Battle of Henkar to facilitate the safe withdrawal of the platoon from Henkar and they were martyred doing so!"

Epilogue

I felt something wet on my face. I sat up startled. I must have dozed off. It was Chow Mein giving my face a nice lick. It was a year since the incident at Henkar and since we found Chow Mein (yes – I had named the ex-Chinese Army Labrador that, and adopted him). I was posted to Army Headquarters, New Delhi six months back and had brought Chow Mein with me. If only he could talk, he could probably tell me with whom he had come, down the path leading to Henkar that night, exactly a year ago; and I wonder if it was really Ranjeet and Ram who saved the day once again a full 50 years hence.

However, before I finally left Henkar, I had a small structure built over the whitewashed stone and a memorial plaque in granite erected for Ranjeet Thapa and Ram Bahadur.

Story **TEN**

BUNGALOW DE INSPEÇÃO CARANZOL

Now I know what a ghost is. Unfinished business, that's what.
-Salman Rushdie, The Satanic Verses

My wife's grand dad was an old railway man – a grizzled veteran of the times when the great Indian Railways were still brown-field, and there were many uncharted trails being blazed by the two parallel lines of steel – mostly by courageous and passionate men who braved the odds, nature and malaria to often deliver the impossible.

Grandpa joined the Southern Railway as a junior engineer in the earlier part of the 20th Century and retired sometime in the 1980s as a Chief Engineer. He was literally a treasure trove of tales from a time bygone – with which he often regaled our evenings.

I remember that particular evening, it was raining cats and dogs as it often does in Pune, and a power outage had plunged our house and locality into darkness. We sat sipping some fine whisky in the veranda, when my wife poked him. "*Tatha*[57], why don't you tell us another good story from your railway days?"

Not that he needed much goading; he always had a great sense of pride talking about his life in the Railway. Taking a swig of the fine scotch, the old man began his tale. Of his many tales, this poignant story he told us that dark night many years ago, has stayed in memory quite vividly.

It was the early 1930s when India was still British India and the beautiful postage-stamp sized territory on India's western coast, known today as the State of Goa, was part of Estado Português da India or the 'Portuguese State of India'. The great Indian Peninsular Railway system was connected the tiny enclave through a single railway line operated by the Southern Maratha Railway on the Indian side, with Castle Rock as the last station, and West of India Portuguese Railway (WIPR) on the Goan side with Caranzol as the first station. The metre gauge line crossed over a 26 km forest covered hill section known as the Braganza Ghat.

I was a junior engineer on my first assignment with the Southern Maratha Railway and was briefly 'loaned' to the WIPR when my employers won a contract to fix this particular critical yet troublesome stretch of track (which was closed for rail traffic now for some time). I was staying at the Railway

[57]Grandfather in Tamil

[58]Refer trivia section for more details.

Dak Bungalow[59] in Castle Rock and would travel everyday with two trusted gang-men on an inspection trolley – a distance of about 8 km to the work site at the railway tunnel at Caranzol. We invariably used to get back before sunset as the area was covered with dense forest and infested with quite ferocious wildlife such as tigers, leopards and bears.

That particular day, there was some critical embankment work in progress, and before we realized, the sun was already waning for the day. To top it all, it started raining quite hard. The labourers had all melted away; I and the two gang men, Munnusamy the senior one and Ahmad the junior one, were the only ones left, drenched to the skin, standing on the lone platform of the run down and unmanned Caranzol[58] Railway Station. Tired and hungry, we decided to find some shelter for the night there itself rather than risking going through the dense jungle back to Castle Rock. Moreover, as the gang-men were also on deputation with me, they too knew very little about the local geography.

We looked around in the darkness for any sign of human habitation around the railway siding. A yellow light flickered some distance away. We squelched through the water covered pathway leading up to the light and ran into a dilapidated gate in the darkness. Munnusamy lit up the gate with light of the inspection lamp; it had a rusty board hanging on it proclaiming quite grandly, 'Bungalow de Inspeção Caranzol' with the logo of WIPR on the top.

"Caranzol Inspection Bungalow!" I translated. "Finally, we will have some place to stay for the night."

The actual building was about 20 yards from the gate, but it was hardly a 'Bungalow'; rather a small stone house with lichen covered walls and a run-down look about it.

"Hello! *Koi hai*![60] " I shouted and motioned the two gang

---

[59]A government rest house in British India

[60]Literally "Anybody there?" in HIndi

men to look around.

They were finally able to locate the source of the light. It emanated from a small outhouse towards the rear of the building. They knocked the door of the outhouse and after a few minutes, we heard feet shuffling inside as the light came closer. The door opened to reveal an unkempt and surly looking man who reeked of cheap liquor. Munnusamy asked him if he was the care taker of the house. He grunted, which we presumed was a "Yes!" When we told him of our intention to stay for the night at the house, much to our annoyance, he flatly refused. "The bungalow is not liveable; it has not been opened for years; it is full of rats, you cannot stay there," he replied in guttural Hindi.

Naturally we declined his hospitable suggestion. I could not take it anymore.

"You draw your wages from the Railway, and yet you refuse to open it for a railway officer!" I screamed. "Let me have no more of nonsense; open up the place at once and get it ready for me, or I shall report you."

The caretaker gave us an evil look, and said, "Okay Sahib," shrugged his shoulders and hobbled away behind the outhouse; as we hoped, to get the key. But after waiting ten minutes I sent Ahmad to search for him. He was nowhere to be found and had apparently decamped down a small path leading into the jungle.

There was nothing to be done now but to break the padlock on the door of the inspection bungalow, which the gang men effected with a stone, and as soon as the door moved slowly back on its hinges we hurried in. It was a dark and damp place and a few resident bats flew right in our faces as we stood in the doorway and tried to make out the interior. The gang men flashed the inspection lamp all around. The room was bare except for a table, chairs, two charpoys, and an old pair of candlesticks. The table and chairs were covered with fungus and the walls were streaked with mouldy green stains. I could not restrain an involuntary shudder as I looked surveyed the unhealthy precincts. Not that we had much of a choice on this dark stormy night.

The gang men were quite efficient as they got a kerosene lantern from the inspection trolley which lit up the room reasonably well. Both of them busied themselves in cleaning up the place and even found an old cotton mattress in the lone wooden cupboard. They quickly cleaned the room and made it at least suitable for me to spend the night.

Thanks to the Railway SOPs[61] (we were expected to carry 48 hours' worth of dry rations and a kerosene stove, when out in the field), the boys were able to cook up a simple yet hot meal in an hour or so and neatly lay it out on the table. After dinner, the gang men cleared the table and retired to rest in the veranda outside.

Before going to bed I decided to explore the next room, a smaller one than the one I occupied. It was empty barring a battered old steel trunk. I opened the truck which revealed an old sola topee or pith hat covered completely with mould, a tiffin carrier and an old diary, which apparently was some kind of a visitor's book. I picked up the diary to read. It might contain something interesting, I wondered. The entries were mostly routine – about who stayed, for how many days, what they paid, etc. However, the comments about the caretaker, both in English and in Portuguese were anything but complimentary.

Streaks of lightning lit up the sky and claps of thunder followed. I glanced at the window – and jumped out of my skin, horribly startled! There was the caretaker peering into the house – his hideous and ugly face was lit up for a moment by the flash of the lightning. I yelled for the gang men and they quickly searched the surroundings for the wretch; but once more he was nowhere to be found.

[61]Standard Operating Procedure

"Sir, he must have run off! We will keep a watch. You don't worry," they reassured me.

It had been a long day and finally I decided to sleep. However, I kept the wick of the lantern at its minimum; so much so, that it threw a faint light around it on the table where it was placed.

I must have dozed off to a fitful sleep, when I was woken up with a bright light falling on my face. I got up groggily and wondered who had turned up the lamp or switched on the inspection light. But when I was fully awake I realized I was mistaken, or was I dreaming?

There was another person in the room! Apparently, another traveller, who appeared to be totally oblivious of my presence and had made himself completely at home. A tiffin carrier, a bed holder (known as a hold-all in railway parlance) lay on the floor next to him. A sola topee was placed on the adjacent chair. I leant up on my elbow and gazed at the intruder in profound amazement. He did not still seem to notice me. Of course, my charpoy was in one corner of the room, but still it would have been impossible for him not to notice my presence.

The stranger was writing a letter at the table facing me. The two candles had been lit and the lantern's light had been turned up, and I could clearly make out his features. He was a young good-looking European, with dark hair. I could not see his eyes, they were bent upon the paper before him; his hands, I noticed, were well shaped and fair with long fingers. He wore a large ring on the ring finger of the left hand, and was well dressed – quite surprising, considering the locale and the awful weather outside.

An old-fashioned leather dispatch bag lay open in front of him. It contained what seemed to be a wallet bulging with currency notes. A golden pocket watch tethered with a chain to his coat pocket shone in the light.

I cleared my throat quite loudly in a polite attempt to

exhibit my presence. However, the gentleman was still unperturbed and continued to write on the paper before him.

Suddenly I realized that the door was ajar and I saw a vaguely familiar face peering inside. It was the caretaker! His gaze seemed riveted on the open dispatch-bag, the wallet and the watch. I wondered how he had come in without rousing the gang men.

Before I realized what was happening, the scoundrel tip toed behind the traveller and drew out a long knife. The traveller raised his eyes and looked at me with a sad melancholy look – almost as if he was seeking my help. I tried to scream as the swarthy man brought down the knife with a swift stroke on the traveller's back. No sound came up from my throat as the traveller fell forward over his letter with a crash and a groan; and all was darkness.

Panic and fear made me break out into a cold sweat as I presumed that the murderer would try to kill me next, as I was an eye-witness to the ghastly act. However, in the darkness there was nothing to be seen. But I could clearly hear the sound of the dragging of a heavy body across the room; then, after a sizeable pause, the sounds of digging outside the bungalow and the splashing of water and mopping – as though someone was cleaning the floor.

Logically, I should have called out for the gang men; but for some reason I apparently went back to sleep again. The next thing I realized was the gang men trying to wake me up. The room was bright.

"Sir, it is almost noon! Are you okay. We got a little worried as you normally do not sleep so late!"

I got up with a start and the look on my face told them something was wrong!

"I have just been witness to a murder. The caretaker murdered a man – a European – in this room, last night!"

Both of them exchanged puzzled glances. "Sir, we have been in the veranda the whole night, taking turns to keep watch. No one was here the whole of last night. You must have had a bad dream!" said Munnusamy.

However, the incident continued to torment me as we went back to the work site at the tunnel. I asked Munnusamy to inquire around. Around lunch time I saw him getting a dark-complexioned old man, apparently a local tribal, to me. The man definitely seemed ill at ease. "Sir! He is Vilas a local wood cutter and has been around these parts for quite some time. When I was inquiring about the bungalow, he started acting strange and was trying to evade my questions. I think he knows something about this."

I came straight to the point and asked him if he knew anything about the bungalow and if something untoward had ever had happened there. The colour seemed to drain from his dark face as he shook his head and turned back. However, the gang men caught him and I questioned him again this time sternly, waving a 2 Rupee note.

"What is there in that house?"

"Evil... The *shaitan*[62] is there!" he said pointing a shaky finger in the general direction of the house.

"Nonsense! There has been a murder; tell the truth!" I retorted.

"I am just a poor wood cutter – I don't know anything!" he wailed.

"A white *sahib* was murdered there, wasn't he?" I glowered at him. "If you don't tell the truth to me I will make sure the police get it from you," I added unsympathetically.

After much threatening and brow beating, we extracted the following information in bits and pieces:

The bungalow was evil, no one ever entered it, and there were lights in the windows every night up to midnight. One day, (so it was said), many years ago, a young sahib came to this bungalow and stayed for around three-four days. He was alone and rode a horse. He was from

---

[62]Devil

the Railway department in Mormugao. The last evening, he retired to bed and was supposed to leave for Mormugao the next morning. Though his people waited for over 20 days, he never appeared, and was never seen again – neither was his horse.

The caretaker declared that the Sahib had left on horseback in the early hours of morning. The police carried out an extensive inquiry and searched the whole area. All they found was the partially devoured carcass of the horse along with the torn trench coat of the Sahib, deep in the forest in the Braganza Ghats. It was presumed that either a leopard or tiger had taken down the unfortunate man and the horse. The case was thus closed.

A couple of years later, the caretaker suddenly became very rich; said he had found a treasure. Also, he had sold a fine gold watch in Colem (the nearest town); and had taken to drinking heavily. He had a bad name, and the bungalow too had a bad name. No one would stay there more than one night, and no one had stayed there for many years till we had come. The caretaker lived in the out-house and he was perpetually drunk.

People said there were shaitans in the house, and no one would go near it after sundown.

This was all he knew.

"So, it was indeed the poor fellow who was murdered and buried at the bungalow! It must have been his hat and tiffin carrier I saw in the trunk!" I exclaimed.

The weather had cleared and we hurried back to Castle Rock. On arrival I immediately sought an appointment with Mr Campbell, my Superintending Engineer, an affable Scot and veteran of the Indian Railways. He appeared quite irritated as it was quite late.

"Ramu, this better be something important…I have had a long day and have a bad migraine."

I rattled out all that I had seen and heard at and about the Inspection Bungalow a Caranzol. His irritation now seemed to turn into amusement.

"Ramu! You Indians are really superstitious. You must

have had a bad dream or had too much of the local arrack!" he said.

"Sir! I don't touch liquor!" I said quite indignantly (Grandpa was a teetotaller those days).

"Why don't you at least pass a message to Panjim to check if anyone ever went missing; as the person I saw was definitely European, and apparently Portuguese, as per the old tribal."

"Okay, I'll speak to someone tomorrow morning. Suggest you go get some sleep. You don't look too good," said Campbell in a surprisingly soft tone.

I do not know who Campbell had called at Panjim; but I got a frantic call around 10 am from him.

"Ramu! Leave for Caranzol immediately. Apparently, a young surveyor had been deputed by WIPR about 8 years back to work on the Caranzol tunnel project (the tunnel came up about 6 years ago). He had travelled from Mormugao to Caranzol on horseback and spent 3-4 days surveying in the Braganza Ghats. He was last seen in Caranzol and was supposed to have left back for Mormugao on his horse; only he never made it back, and was not found ever since, in spite of the police launching a search. Your description seems to match him…they are sending a police party up to Caranzol."

The gang men and I hurried to Caranzol on the inspection trolley. We found half a dozen Goan Askaris and a Portuguese police officer already there waiting for us. They had got a few local coolies with digging tools. On the basis of my description, they began digging under the steps in the front of the house while we waited in the house. Soon, one of the coolies came running. His expression said it all. The remains of the surveyor had been found!

Francisco Silva, the Portuguese Officer, had known the surveyor, Amâncio Gracias – a promising young man who had arrived a few weeks back from Lisbon. In the same grave was found the battered dispatch-bag and a large ring on the left ring finger by which the skeleton was identified. Silva and the policemen re-interred the body under a banyan tree, and read the Burial Service over it, made a makeshift tomb stone and planted a wooden cross over it.

From what I heard thereafter, the caretaker was thoroughly searched for by the Goan and Indian police. He was never found. He seemed to have just vanished from that part of the country, and was presumed to have been devoured by a tiger in the jungles; but that was too good to be true. I believe the unfortunate young man's relations back in Portugal, were eventually informed of the discovery of his remains and the dispatch-bag and ring were sent to them.

As Campbell felt that the episode had been very traumatic for me, he had me immediately repatriated back to my parent railway, far away from Castle Rock or Caranzol and I never went anywhere near that geography in my entire career after that. I came to know a few years down the line that the old Portuguese bungalow at Caranzol had been pulled down to make way for a new siding for watering the steam locos hauling coal to the Port of Mormugao.

Suddenly the lights came on as the power had been restored. My wife and I were shaken out of the trance this melancholic tale had put us into…

Grandpa motioned to his empty glass and said, "Son! Why don't you get me a refill?"

Story ELEVEN

FOR HIS GLORY

May no ill dreams disturb my rest,
nor Powers of Darkness me molest
—Evening Hymn

Devarshola, The Nilgiris, South India, September 2018

A late 80s black Ambassador car slowly chugged up a rutted path opposite the ruined church leading up to the old school compound, deep in the Nilgiri Mountains in South India. John Arokiaraj, 65, sitting in the backseat, gazed at the decayed building and exclaimed. "My God, look at it!"

Shards of stained glass still hung from the windows though vegetation had taken over the old stone walls. Rusted metal letters near the front door identified the place as 'Mar

Thoma Church 1867'.

Ramesh in his early 30s, at the wheel, cast eyes to the rear-view mirror as he drove past and asked John, "Uncle, when was the last time you were here?"

"1961 – The year...it all happened…" said John ruefully.

Rosie, 42, sitting at the co-driver's seat squinted her eyes as she spotted a one storey brick building and said, "Ah! That must be the old school."

John said, "That's right. That was my second standard classroom there," pointing to a broken window on the near wall.

They finally reached their destination – a two-storey stone house at the end of the road. Overgrown ivy covered the walls, and the compound was thick with bushes and scrub.

Ramesh stepped out of the car, stared at the house and said, "I think we are there – this should be the convent."

Rosie too got out of the car, surveyed the convent, walked to the front door and gently touched her fingertips to the faded and weather-beaten oak door.

Ramesh walked back to the boot of the car, and pulled out a folded wheelchair and a large bag. John opened his door as Ramesh rolled the wheelchair up to him. He groaned as he swung himself into the seat.

"Problems of old age, kid."

Ramesh smiled, and pushed John to the front door. They saw Rosie slowly sliding her fingers across the door. Ramesh gave her a questioning look.

Rosie said, "I feel energy, fierce energy."

Ramesh looked at the broken lock on the door, grasped the brass handle and pushed it open. Dusk had given way to night and the darkness set in suddenly, as it typically happens in the hills. Ramesh pushed John in, then reached into his backpack, pulled out a Maglite and switched it on. Rosie too switched on the flashlight on her mobile phone. The two LED beams cut through the darkness. Decades of grime, dust and cobwebs covered everything. Ramesh passed his light over an old coat rack and Rosie bent down and picked a yellowed piece of newspaper off the floor. The date read 'September 5th, 1961'. She tossed it to the floor and muttered something under her breath.

John rolled himself to a wall near the staircase and switched on his mobile phone's torch too. A large framed photograph hung there. He wiped the thick layer of dust with his hand and gasped and staggered when he saw the face looking back from the frame and exclaimed, "Oh my God! It's her!"

Ramesh walked over, and saw a black and white photo of a middle-aged nun in a habit. The name beneath her photo read: '*Sister Mary Balderston*'. Ramesh wiped the rest of the dust off. The heading of the frame said: '*The Sisters of Mar Thoma Convent welcome you.*' Beneath the countenance of Sister Mary were smaller photos of eight other nuns. John stared at the photo of Sister Mary and a shiver ran down his spine.

Mar Thoma Convent, the Nilgiris, September 1961

An eight-year-old John sat at his desk in the classroom. He and the other children sat in petrified silence as Sister Mary Balderston walked up and down the rows. Such was the fear she instilled in him, that he did not even look up. He instead glanced out of the window.

"Johnny! Pay attention to the class!" shouted Sister Mary in a thick Scottish accent as she rapped his knuckles with a wooden foot-ruler.

Mar Thoma Convent, the Nilgiris, 9:30 P.M., 5th September 2018

John rubbed his rubbed his right knuckles with his left hand.

Ramesh looked at him ruefully and said, "Uncle, hope you are fine! You sure you want to be here?"

John shook his head and said, "I'm fine. Been a long while… Some memories were just rewinding."

Rosie looked around, aimed her light to the first floor and muttered ominously, "Whatever's here...it's aware of us. I don't know…but I get the feeling that we are being watched."

Thunder claps and lightning played merry outside followed by a downpour. The three looked at each other nervously in the beam of the flashlights.

Ramesh broke the pregnant silence by shouting over the thunder claps, "Okay…let's get started on what we came here for!"

Ramesh picked up his video camera in one hand and an EM sensor in the other. He then turned the camera onto himself.

"Okay, this is Ramesh of the Ghost Hunters Society, along with psychic Rosie Matthews. It's September 5th, 2018 around 9:30 p.m. We're here at the Mar Thoma convent, the Nilgiris, the site of a mass suicide by nine nuns back in 1961. The nuns were led by Sister Mary Balderston, whose ghost supposedly haunts this place. For years, witnesses claimed to have seen a black figure passing by windows and walking the grounds of the church and school. The locals don't dare to venture near this place, even in broad day light!"

Ramesh then turned the camera to John and said, "We're so lucky to have Mr. John Arokiaraj with us. Uncle John was a student at the time of the suicides and this is his first time back here since then."

John smiled back nervously into the camera.

"John Sir, what can you tell us about Sister Mary?" asked Ramesh.

"Sister Mary was a terror, not that the other nuns were anything great; but she just seemed to revel in tormenting us. She would slap us, beat us, cane us and this is what originally opened up the investigation," said John.

"From what I remember, some parents went to the cops when they found bruises and welts on their children. That's when it was found how depraved things really were here," added Ramesh.

"…seems you have done your research well!" said John.

They then walked into the kitchen. Ramesh shone his flashlight around the empty cupboards.

"Sir, I know it was a long time ago, but do you remember your thoughts when you first learned of the possible practice of black magic and devil worship here at Mar Thoma?" asked Ramesh.

"I didn't really understand it. I do remember my parents whispering about it. The whole town was like that; people would discuss matters in hushed tones," said John.

Rosie rubbed her arms with her hands as it had started getting cold and gazed at the ceiling.

John continued "…and then, next thing you know the Diocese shuts the school and church down. They just abandoned it. Let it rot away, like a bad memory you want to forget."

There was a loud crash from the foyer and the three jumped out of their skins. Ramesh and Rosie ran toward the noise and John followed on the wheel chair.

The coat rack lay shattered on the floor. They looked around the room and Ramesh bent down to inspect the rack. One of the three legs seemed to have broken off. Ramesh quickly pulled out the EM sensor and took a reading but the sensor did not show any electromagnetic disturbance at all.

"Probably one of the legs on this rack was loose and it crashing now might be just co-incidence," said Ramesh shaking his head.

Rosie raised her hand.

"No. Something is here. It's with us."

Ramesh looked up, and seeing the concern in her eyes said, "Okay, let's check the basement too!"

Ramesh and Rosie gingerly entered the basement through the old stairs. John reluctantly agreed to stay at the door to the basement as he would not be able to use the rickety stairway leading downwards. Black paint peeled from the walls and ceiling. Ramesh rubbed his shoe on the dirty floor. The dust parted to reveal what must have been a red flooring. Rosie clenched her eyes shut and began breathing heavily.

Within the basement, eight nuns stand in a large circle with Sister Mary in the middle. Each of them holds a butcher knife. A seven-edged star – the Septenary Sigil lit by candles at each edge, shines out of the bright red floor. Sister Mary exclaims: "For his glory!" With that, Sister Mary and the nuns slit their own throats.

Rosie opened her eyes, and staggered back to the wall, drenched in a cold sweat. In the meantime, John who was at the hallway and heard what sounded like a long exhale.

Then... A plaintive female voice called out in a hoarse whisper – "John!"

John whipped his head towards the entrance and whipped out a black revolver which he had worn in a holster inside his jacket. Cocking it's hammer he shouted into the darkness, "Who the fuck is it? I will blow your freaking brains out!"

Ramesh rubbed Rosie on the shoulder and gave her a questioning glance.

"I saw them all!" said Rosie as she dropped to her knees and frantically pushed dirt away. The faded black lines of the heptagram begin to appear. Ramesh too struck his EM sensor in his front pocket, dropped to his knees and brushed away dirt.

The rain had stopped and bright moonlight streamed in through the windows and skylights. John felt all the more nervous and uncomfortable and rolled himself into the foyer and stared uneasily at the photo of Sister Mary.

In the meantime, Ramesh and Rosie uncovered most of the symbol, including the goat-headed Baphomet image in the centre. Rosie's breathing started becoming ragged. She steadied herself against a wall and clenched her eyes shut again.

Sister Mary watches as Father Maurice, a young priest, descends the basement staircase. Seven nuns stand around the Septenary Sigil. A young nun stands on a side and strips off her clothes. The Priest too takes off all his clothes and advances into the circle. Sister Mary grins fiendishly as she watches the priest and nun fornicate inside the satanic symbol.

Rosie groaned and gasped as she broke from the vision.

"The priest… Father Maurice…" she murmured.

Ramesh looked at her and asked, "Was he was the one who began the satanic rituals?"

"No… It was Mary. She was the true evil; the root of all the corruption. All she wanted was to defile God."

Rosie caught her breath, looked at a heavy wooden table that stood against the far wall. She approached it and ran her hands all over it. A look of confusion and horror spread across her face and she whispered, "There is something more," bringing her hands to her eyes.

Sister Mary, Father Maurice and seven nuns watch as the pregnant nun lay on the floor squirming in pain. The young nun's screaming reaches a crescendo and then she suddenly calms down as she manages to push out the baby. Sister Mary quickly snatches it up, slices the umbilical cord and carries the baby to the wooden table at the far wall. A black muslin cloth covers the table. She places the new born on the make-shift altar and picks up an axe lying next to it. She breaks out into a demonic laughter as she raises the axe.

Rosie let out a loud scream. "Oh God! She didn't spare any one!" and ran to the other end of the room and knocked the wall – as though to check for hollowness.

She motioned Ramesh to help her break a portion of the wall. A resounding kick ensured a gaping hole in the false wall. Rosie flashed her torch into the hole and peered inside. She fell back; gagged and choked with terror and turned around and ran out of the basement. A terrified Ramesh then shone his flashlight into the hidden room. There were at least ten tiny skeletons on the floor neatly set in a row!

Rosie ran past John and towards the front door of the

building. The door suddenly slammed shut. She tugged the handle and tried to open the door – but it did not budge.

She yelled hysterically, "She is still here and won't spare us! The evil here is unspeakable!" In desperation, Rosie ran upstairs.

John was stunned and stammered, "R…Rosie…! What happened…!?" and gripped the revolver tightly and a cold sweat drenched the back of his neck.

Not answering him, Rosie ran down the hallway on the first floor and suddenly jerked to a halt. At the other end of the hallway stood a black figure. Her silhouette suggested an old-fashioned nun's robe. Rosie reached out for the nearest door and crawled inside the dark room.

Ramesh ran into the foyer, nearly falling over John.

"We have to get out now!" said John. He knew instinctively that something was wrong; and Rosie's actions, and the history of the place told him it was imperative that they leave.

Ramesh gripped the knob of the front door, trying in vain to open it.

"Where's Rosie?" asked Ramesh.

"She ran upstairs...as though she had seen a ghoul!" said John.

Ramesh dropped his gear on the floor and ran upstairs.

"Ramesh! We have to get out!" screamed John as he rolled his wheelchair to the door and twisted the knob.

Rosie crawled away from the door and got to her feet. She shone the flashlight around and spotted a window. Rosie kicked the window attempting to open it, but it was jammed. There was a large closet at the other end of the room. She gingerly opened the closet. There were a number of nun's robes covered in an inch of mildew. On the top shelf, she spotted the wooden handle of what appeared to be an axe. A chill passed down her spine as she realized that she was most probably in Sister Mary's bedroom closet!

Suddenly an infernal shadow entered the room and in

spite of the flashlight, enveloped the walls in darkness as it moved toward Rosie. Rosie grabbed the axe and scurried to a corner. The ghoulish figure of Sister Mary appeared before her. Rosie's mouth dropped and eyes widened in abject trepidation.

Ramesh threw open every door as he ran across the hallway on the first floor, looking frantically for Rosie. He reached the door leading to Sister Mary' bedroom and tried the knob but it did not budge.

Ramesh shouted, "Rosie! Are you there?"

He then pressed his ear to the door and heard a shuffling noise. In panic, he frantically kicked at the door and it finally gave way. Ramesh stared ahead in the light of his torch, frozen in fear at what his eyes beheld. The EM sensor in his pocket went berserk emitting a high-pitched whine.

As John struggled with the front door, he heard the noises of a struggle upstairs and then the sound of a body thumping to the floor.

"Ramesh! Rosie! Where are you?" John shouted.

Only to be greeted by silence.

He then heard slow, deliberate footsteps from the first floor and the wooden floor creaking. The footsteps then, began to descend the stairway. John watched in horror as a woman in a blood-splattered nun's dress walked down the stairs. The axe she held glistened with fresh blood in the moonlight creeping through the window. John rolled backward into a wall, quivering with fear. He raised his revolver and opened fire on the figure. The apparition however continued to move towards him.

Finally, the hammer of the revolver clicked ineffectively as he ran out of bullets. The figure then turned its head towards John and grinned at him. She strangely looked like Rosie! In place of eyes, she had two black holes.

A surreal voice which took him back many years said in a thick Scottish accent, "Johnny! Pay attention in the class!"

as the figure swung the axe and beheaded him in one stroke.

Rosie then stepped away and lifted the blade of the axe to her own throat and screamed, "For his glory!" as she slit it across.

The arterial spray coated the walls. A moment later, she dropped to the floor. Drops of blood created patterns as they splashed on the black and white photograph of Sister Mary Balderston hung on the wall.

Mahabaleshwar, Western India, May 2019

The credits begun rolling in –

'In order of appearance: -

John Arokiaraj .... *Ajit Murudkar*
Sister Mary .... *Johanna Thomas*
Ramesh .... *Ashok Ganapathy*
Rosie .... *Manisha Kalra'*

Ajit got up and switched off the TV. He had a satisfied smile. His 'Horror Nights' TV show had made him a celebrity overnight; but he had to admit that shooting this episode had given him the creeps, considering that the tale of the ritual suicide of the nuns of Mar Thoma in 1961 was indeed a true story, though the rest was based on local folk lore and urban legend.

It was past midnight. He yawned as he loped off towards the bedroom of his ancestral house in Mahabaleshwar where he lived alone after his divorce from Kavita a couple of years back. It was raining heavily outside, so typical of Mahabaleshwar. Suddenly the power went off. Also, very typical of this weather.

As a matter of habit, he picked up the candlestick with a half-burnt candle perched on it from the wooden side board and lit it with his cigarette lighter. The yellow light flickered as he walked to his room.

The thunder crashed outside and the candle went out due to a draft of cold air – probably through some open window – he thought. He then heard a vaguely familiar female voice calling out in a whisper, "Johnny!" from behind him.

"What the hell!" he exclaimed as he instinctively turned around.

The cold steel of an axe-head plunged into his chest and the last visual he had as he collapsed was a dark shadow in a nun's habit and a ghoulish voice exclaiming "*For his glory*!"

Story **TWELVE**

7, THE MALL

Believe only half of what you see
and nothing that you hear.
-Edgar Allan Poe

The dank smell of mould and bat offal was overpowering. Kaizaad covered his mouth and nose with a handkerchief and Ram Din, the old chowkidar nervously led him into the cavernous interiors of the mansion. In the dim light of the lantern and some ambient light permeating through the dusty blinds hanging over the windows, he could make out antiquated furniture including what looked like old sofas (with in explicable dark brown stains and holes in them), a long dining table and a wreck of a piano lying in what appeared to be the main dining area of the house.

The chowkidar nervously pointed his finger towards a

flight of wooden stairs which lead to the first floor.

"We need to go up there!" he said in a slightly quivering voice. "Sahib! Do you really want to stay here…?" he asked nervously. "This place is no good!"

Kaizaad and Darius exchanged glances.

"Kaizaad… Do you really want to do this?" asked Darius in a low voice.

"Of course! I think we already discussed this Dari," said Kaizaad putting the conversation to rest and they trudged up the creaky old stairs.

The audience once used to only mythological and historical films, had lapped up the action flicks of Mary Ann Evans a.k.a Fearless Nadia produced and directed by Homi Wadia, whose muse she was rumoured to be. The Indian audience was now mature enough to appreciate new genres of films…and horror was a brand-new genre in Indian films. He wanted to be the Indian equivalent of Lon Chaney and Bela Lugosi – the Hollywood stars who had become superstars starring in Horror movies.

Kaizaad had lapped up all the movies of the two actors, and realized that the realistic way to play a character expressively was through identifying with, understanding, and experiencing a character's inner motivation and emotions. Most Indian actors were still struck in the old-fashioned stage method of acting – he badly wanted to break the mould. His last movie- 'Jailor' released 8 months ago, in June 1938 (also directed by Darius Mody, his childhood friend, and one of India's top contemporary movie directors) was a blockbuster mainly due to Kaizaad's realistic portrayal of a sadistic jailor. He had spent a month in Poona's Yerawada Jail – observing every move of the jailor, his mannerisms, language etc.; and was thereby able to pull off his titular role in the movie with aplomb. Thanks to this role, was Kaizaad Mehta now known as India's only method actor.

His thoughts were interrupted with the old chowkidar

tapping him on the shoulder as he shone the light into the room where Kaizaad planned to spend the night. Darius moved and pushed aside the dusty curtain which let the evening light come in. The chowkidar had somewhat cleaned up the room which consisted of an old four-poster cot on which a bed roll had been placed. Apart from that an old wooden wardrobe (in shambles) and an antiquated dresser with a mirror (whose silver coating had worn off) and a small peg table (on which the old man had placed an earthen pot with drinking water and a steel tumbler) also occupied the room. The chowkidar lit up an oil lamp and placed it on the dresser. He still appeared very nervous and seemed eager to go.

After a lot of scouting Darius and Kaizaad had found this old, grand yet run down mansion in Cawnpore , which seemed to fit the bill completely for the yet untitled movie of Darius Mody, touted to be India's first horror magnum opus. The mansion had apparently been locked up since 1857 as no one wanted to live there. Not only were locals scared to come anywhere near it, even British Administrators and government officials gave it a pass. Probably its painful past had something to do with it.

The Bungalow at 7, The Mall, Civil Lines, used to be the residence of Sir Hugh Wheeler , the Garrison Commander of Cawnpore during the Sepoy Mutiny of 1857. Whilst he was killed in action in Satichaura Ghat, Lady Wheeler and their daughters along with a number of other European women and children had been brutally massacred in this very house allegedly by a courtesan named Hussaini Khanum and a few Sepoys.

Kaizaad came down the stairs with Darius and the chowkidar, and came till the main door with them. It was almost 7:30 in the evening, and darkness was settling in. Darius looked at Kaizaad once again.

Sensing his discomfort Kaizaad said, "Dari, I am fine.

See you for breakfast at the Circuit House in the morning."

"Okay, will send Ram Din to fetch you at 7 AM sharp," said Darius waving him good night.

Darius had offered to stay with Kaizaad, but he was adamant to stay alone to get a true 'feel' of the place.

The old chowkidar seemed very relieved as he and Darius left the precincts of the house. It had been a tiring day and the heavy lunch and one too many gins with tonic at the lunch hosted by Craig Thomas, the Superintendent of Police for their movie crew had made Kaizaad tired and drowsy. He decided to hit the bed right away. Tomorrow was a long day of shoots in any case.

Darius had planned the night shoot at the house after a couple of days, post wrapping up the day shoots, which gave Kaizaad enough time to soak up the melancholic atmosphere of the house.

He walked up the stairs and reached the bedroom. He shut the door and latched it. He then turned the wick of the lamp to its lowest so that only a little light emanated from it and lay down on the bed. He could hear the distant sound of a clock tower chiming eight times and slowly drifted off to sleep.

Kaizaad got up with a jerk. Something had disturbed him. It was still dark and the oil lamp threw a small halo of yellow light around it.

"Must have been the scurrying of a rat or something," he thought as he tried to go back to sleep. He could hear the distant clock tower – he counted 12 chimes. It was midnight.

He was almost asleep when he heard a knock on the door of the room. He sat up on the bed.

"I must be dreaming," he muttered to himself. There was no one in the house barring him. But the knock repeated itself quite distinctly and more purposefully this time. Now Kaizaad was worried. "Must be Ram Din. Darius must have sent him to check out on me," he thought and called out

"Who's it?"

To his surprise he heard a reply in quite a refined voice "Sir, everyone is waiting for you down stairs. Please join for supper."

"What the hell…? Ram Din, Dari… Is it you people…? is this some kind of a joke?" shouted Kaizaad in a nervous voice.

In response the knock repeated itself and the voice said "Sir, you cannot make the ladies wait."

Kaizaad was now a little scared but more irritated as he went up to the door and after unlatching, opened it. A smart looking European in antiquated liveries stood in front of him. He smiled at him and said, "Sir, we are all waiting for you!"

The interiors of the house were brightly lit with a multitude of lamps and the house looked spic and span. Kaizaad could hear the chatter of a number of people speaking down stairs along with the clatter of crockery and some indistinct tune playing on the piano.

As though in a trance Kaizaad followed the liveried butler down the passageway and down the stairs. The hall was brightly lit with crockery neatly laid out on the long dining table. There were at least 25-30 people on the hall and as he walked down the stairs a few of them looked at him and smiled. An aristocratic lady sat on the sofa and a pretty young girl played the piano.

A couple of young officers in old fashioned military regalia were hovering around the girl. One of them was particularly handsome with blond hair and sharp features. A shiny medal dangling on a blue piece of satin adorned his chest.

Suddenly there was a crashing sound outside the house and he could hear yelling and what sounded like gunshots outside. He could sense panic in the gathering, as people ran helter-skelter. Suddenly the door burst open and about 3-4 native soldiers in tattered uniforms burst in brandishing swords and muskets. The blond-haired young officer stood near Kaizaad with his sword drawn; though he seemed oblivious to the Actor's presence. Kaizaad could only watch in horror as one of the native soldiers let go a volley from his musket at the officer. The officer bore the full impact of the buck shot on his chest and came down crashing with a yell; and in the process collided with Kaizaad. Kaizaad lost balance and crashed down as well, banging his head against the edge of the dining table.

Kaizaad got up with a throbbing headache. He was in the bed in his room. Apparently, it was day break and he could again hear the distant clock tower chiming – 7 counts this time. He got up groggily and tried to recollect what had happened last night. He unlocked the room and looked outside. Everything was as run-down and despondent as it was when he first came to the bungalow.

"I must have been dreaming…" he muttered.

He quickly went down the stairs, gingerly looking at the surroundings. The piano, the dining table, the sofa stood the way they had been with inches of dust and grime piled on them.

Ram Din was waiting outside. On seeing Kaizaad he seemed quite relieved that he did not have to enter the house to wake Kaizaad up.

"What happened Sahib?" asked Ram Din inquiringly pointing to the dirt marks on Kaizaad's pants and shirt.

Startled Kaizaad looked down and saw dust caking his dress as though he had fallen down somewhere.

"Damn, I must have been sleep walking," thought Kaizaad.

They walked down to the Circuit House where he found Darius and another crew member sitting outside in the lawn. Darius waved to him.

"I'll just freshen up and join you for breakfast," said Kaizaad.

After quick ablutions, Kaizaad met Darius and Davit, the Armenian cameraman at the breakfast table.

"So, how was the night...? Ram Din told me told me you fell down or something. Hope you are fine," asked Darius.

Kaizaad narrated what he had experienced during the night; but also concluded that he must have been dreaming and must have sleep walked. "After all I woke up on my bed in the morning. Guess I had one too many drinks during the day," he concluded.

Buster, Kaizaad's pet German Shepard came and rubbed itself against his legs and he affectionately tickled the dog behind its ears.

The crew was busy the whole day with shoots. They finished the day with an excellent dinner hosted at Cawnpore Club in the Cantonment. After they got back to the Circuit House, Kaizaad called Ram Din and got ready to go back to spend the night at the old bungalow.

"Sahib! I beg you not to go…that place is evil! You are lucky you came back alive after last night!" pleaded Ram Din.

"Kaizaad, I think you should listen to him or at least let me come with you," added Darius.

"Don't worry Dari. I will be fine and I definitely need to go tonight. I have still not got a complete feel of the house… and tonight I'm not alone. I'm taking along Buster with me and also this…" said Kaizaad showing Darius a shiny revolver which he had tucked in his waistband.

"Just be careful Kaizu…that's all I can say," said Darius, looking rather concerned.

Kaizaad and Ram Din reached the house in a short while. As usual Ram Din was very uneasy and this time, bid goodbye to Kaizaad at the gate itself. Kaizaad and Buster walked into the house and up the creaky stars into the room where Kaizaad lit up the lamp. He picked up the lamp and whispered to Buster, "Let's explore the house a little before we hit the bed!"

"Sahib! Sahib…! Please get up!"

It was the khansamah of the Circuit House banging at

the door of Darius' room. Darius checked his watch. It was 6 AM in the morning. He rubbed his eyes and opened the door. He instinctively knew something was seriously wrong. The khansamah stood ashen faced and behind him stood Craig Thomas the SP and a couple of other policemen.

"What happened?" asked Darius.

"You need to come with me Darius…can't tell you anything now," said Craig in a low voice.

They bundled into his car and in a few minutes pulled up in front of 7, The Mall. A foreboding gripped Darius as he saw a few people already gathered there apart from a couple of policemen. Ram Din too was sitting in a corner crying.

"Ram Din had come in the morning to pick up Kaizaad and he was the one who found Kaizaad and his dog," said Craig as he led Darius inside the house. The curtains had been pulled open and Darius saw Kaizaad and Buster both motionless lying at the foot of the staircase.

Kaizaad's mouth was half open and his eyes clearly described some unspeakable terror. His revolver was still in his right hand with his finger on the trigger.

"Wha…what's wrong with them?" asked Darius.

"I'm sorry; both are dead," said Craig.

"Kaizaad fired all six rounds from his revolver," he continued pointing to bullet marks on the opposite wall. "Surprisingly, there are no visible injury marks on either him or the dog and no sign of anybody else's footprints or signs of a struggle."

One of the policemen came up to Craig and said, "Sir, we found this in the dog's mouth – apparently it bit this off from somewhere or from someone."

Craig shone his flashlight on the object. It appeared to be a military medal of some kind – 'Anglo-Sikh War 1849' was inscribed on it and it was attached to a piece of blue satin. For an artefact so old, the medal surprisingly seemed new and shiny.

Story **THERTEEN**

A LADLE FULL OF REMORSE

[*Dread remorse when you are tempted to err,*
Miss Eyre; remorse is the poison of life.
- Charlotte Brontë, Jane Eyre]

The heat was intolerable as the ladle moved on its rails and emptied itself of molten iron ore with a whoosh into the furnace. Iswar winced as a hot blast of air hit his sweat soaked body. It was not as if this was new to him. He had been working in this oldest of steel plants of Western Steel Industries for the last 15 years. It was a surprise how his lungs held out so far with so much of fine coal dust – which practically covered everything in the vicinity of the plant.

But since the incident of 25th January last year, for some

reason he could feel the extreme elements around him in the steel plant more vividly; be it the heat of the furnace, the glare of the molten metal or the soot and gloomy ambience everywhere. Kamal had been his buddy – both used to practically have lunch together every day – a sparse meal of rotis, onion and salt; but Kamal's gregarious presence and vulgar jokes somehow made lunch hour something he looked forward to everyday. But 25th January had swallowed him and the two poor young lads (Iswar didn't even know their names).

But it was not about Kamal and the two other deaths – it was about how they had died. The furnace had punctured and spattered the surroundings with a spray of molten steel. Most had escaped, but not Kamal and the two lads. They were the nearest to the furnace, guiding the ladle. Kamal was the oldest Foreman in the plant and the most confident and this he had been doing for years. Probably it was his confidence that cost him his life.

Iswar could not forget his 10-minute journey from the plant to the Company medical centre in the ambulance, with what appeared to be three slabs of meat. The 1600-degree Centigrade molten steel did not give them a chance; the skin had vaporized and the underlying tissues had cooked. The good part was they could feel no pain and the bad part was that they were still alive. Iswar remembered Kamal looking at him through his left eye (the right one was gone) and a large tear drop fall off it.

They did not even last half an hour considering the magnitude of the burns. Mr Jain, the owner of the plant was there, as was Chandu the leader of the Workers Union. Iswar heard Chandu shouting in Gujarati – he overhead fragments of the conversation.

"This plant was due for maintenance 2 years back… management kept running it without basic safety…all that matters for them is money and not workmen's lives…we will go to courts…media…get Jain arrested!"

Iswar then saw Jain's secretary trying to calm down Chandu and then lead him to Mr Jain's car. Chandu entered the car and after a few minutes emerged after what seemed to be a brief conversation with the factory owner. Apparently, something significant had been discussed, since Chandu came out looking very purposeful and quietly dispersed the crowds in no time.

The rest passed as though in a daze. Chandu calling him, two other workmen and Ashok the Security Guard, giving them a wad of currency each and also veiled threats. The three bodies were disposed of by burying them deep below the scrap yard in the factory and then piling up tonnes of scrap metal on top. Of course, Jain would have taken care of the Factory Inspector by stuffing his mouth with money and paid off a pittance to the emaciated families of the three dead workmen to buy their silence.

It was probably generations of suppression and subservience that made him and the other three act the way they did. But since that night, Iswar was a haunted man – haunted by guilt, haunted by remorse and haunted by pain. He felt he had been grossly disloyal to his only friend. But tonight, it was getting unbearable…probably since in one day's time it was going to be one year since that ghastly accident.

The siren had gone off at 11 P.M. and his shift was over. He was just winding up and wiping the sweat off his brow. The others had already left the furnace shed and he was all alone. Suddenly, he saw a movement on the platform over the furnace.

"Why would anybody walk there when the furnace is live…?" he wondered. The platform was used only during plant maintenance. He winced his eyes to see clearly. There was a hazy figure standing there – he could not make out anything beyond that, as the platform was quite dark.

But he almost fainted when he heard a familiar voice.

"Iswar, Iswar…come here!"

As though in a trance Iswar went closer…he swore it was Kamal, the same rotund face and bright orange safety hat. He grabbed a flashlight and gingerly climbed the ladder to reach the top of platform. There was no one there. He looked around once more. "I must have been dreaming," he muttered and turned to go back when he heard a gurgling sound behind him.

He spun around and shone the flash light.

There were three figures standing two yards away from him – three hideous forms with no skin and only charred flesh and bones through which some gross bodily fluids seemed to be oozing out.

"Don't go Iswar…" said one of them in an unearthly yet pitiable voice. "Help us…! For we are trapped here forever… and you too are responsible for it…"

"What do you want of me! I am sorry for what I did...and I have been regretting it every moment ever since. I have been living in hell for the last one year!" blurted out Iswar.

"Deliver us Jain and Chandu…that will be deliverance for us as well as you," said the figure.

Iswar must have fainted; for when he woke up he was in the medical centre. Chandu was standing next to him.

"What the hell were you doing on the platform…? You could have died. Lucky for you that the security guard noticed you going up and summoned the others to get you down. Don't you know tomorrow is the inauguration of the new furnace by the Legislator? Mr Jain will be there. I don't want any nonsense happening here again!" he said rather gruffly.

The next noon was the inauguration of the new furnace which had replaced the worn-out furnace which had ruptured and caused the accident last year. It was installed next to the currently used furnace and utilised the same ladle set-up for feed of molten metal. What was discussed in whispers at the workmen's canteen was that this furnace too was not new but a refurbished one bought cheaply by Jain.

Chandu made it a point to keep only himself and a few of his cronies in the inner circle with Jain and the dignitaries who had come for the inauguration and lined up the others outside the shed in the blistering sunlight. They could see the small group stand near the furnace, hear the clapping sound as the Legislator pressed the button, and the ladle slowly moved on the rails ready to pour the molten metal into the furnace.

Suddenly there was a grating noise and then the crunching sound of metal buckling. They could only watch in horror as the guiding mechanism of the ladle suddenly seemed to buckle under its weight and instead of the ladle going up to the furnace to empty its contents- suddenly toppled and poured its contents right over the small group standing next to the furnace.

It took a whole day for the molten metal to cool down before they could cut through it to reach whatever remains were left of Chandu, Jain, the Legislator and the others.

A team of government investigators swooped over the plant and all the workmen were quizzed. Iswar told them about the incident last year too. They exhumed the bodies of Kamal and the other two workmen and Iswar performed their last rites. The plant was sealed as it was declared unsafe.

Iswar decided to go back home to his village in Bihar with the little savings he had. Ashok the security guard too was travelling back with him. The train had just left the platform.

"Who were you speaking to that night…? I saw you climb up the platform and it looked as though you were speaking to someone…only I could not see anyone else. I called out for you too…but you didn't seem to hear," said Ashok suddenly.

Iswar was taken aback by the question.

"I…I don't remember anything…I must have walked up to check something and then I fainted I think…" he blurted.

"But then you walked back up to the control room of the ladle…and tinkered with something there and then you fainted as you were trying to come back down through the platform. I didn't tell anything to anyone… I also deleted the CCTV footage before the investigators came in," said Ashok.

"I do not remember any of this! And why didn't you report me in in case you feel I had something to do with what happened on the day of the inauguration?"

Ashok just smiled and said, "Don't worry, Kamal was my friend too; and you are not the only one he'd been talking to of late."

TRIVIA

Sharvara

Sharavara is the fearsome four eyed, wide nostrilled, insatiable mythical dog from Hindu mythology, whose master is Yama - the Hindu God of death. It is one of the two dogs of Yama which guard the gates of hell (*Naraka*). Sharvara is identified with the constellation Canis Major and Sarama the other dog, with Canis Minor.

Thugs

The English word thug traces its roots to a word in HIndi, which means 'cheat' or 'deceiver'. According to the conventional account of *Thuggee* (the collective word for the acts carried out by thugs), they were a fraternity of ritual stranglers who preyed upon travellers along the highways of 19th century India. Their unsuspecting victims were first deceived into joining the thugs and later at some secluded spot they strangled the travellers with a handkerchief or noose, robbed them and buried the body- in a sense, a clean criminal act. During the 1840s, a number of anti-thugee expeditions were led by Colonel (later Major General) William Henry Sleeman of the Bengal Army which effectively suppressed these organised criminal gangs.

Karuppu Rayan

Kapruppu Rayan, also referred to as Karuppasamy, Periya Karuppa Sami, or Malayala Karuppu is an ancient (probably pre-Vedic) male deity popular amongst rural groups in Tamil Nadu. The form of Karuppu Rayan is characterised by bulbous eyes, huge moustaches and fearsome looking teeth. Generally, an annual festival is held at Karuppu Rayan shrines based on local traditions where goats and chicken are sacrificed. Unconventional offerings such as *beedis*, cigarettes and alcohol are made in some of these shrines by devotees.

The Gaisal Train Disaster

The Gaisal train disaster occurred at about 1:45 am on 2 August 1999, when two trains- Avadh Assam Express & Brahmaputra Mail carrying approximately 2,500 people collided at the remote station of Gaisal, Uttar Dinajpur, West Bengal, approximately 19 kilometres from Kishanganj Station. The crash involved such high speeds that the trains exploded upon impact, killing at least 290 people. It is considered to be one of the worst rail disasters in Indian history.

The Patharughat Massacare

Twenty-five years before the Jallianwallah Bagh massacre of 1919, more than a hundred peasants fell to the bullets of the British on January 28, 1894 in Assam. The unarmed peasants were protesting against the increase in land revenue and taxes levied by the colonial administration, when the police opened fire.

Today a 'martyrs column' stands where the incident took place – Patharughat, a small village in Assam's Darrang district, 60km northeast of Guwahati.

Dak Bungalows

In the year 1774, Robert Clive first set up a regular postal system in India and the first bungalows built to relay the post or 'dak'. Quickly, they became a network for the men who ruled India as they toured the districts.

Dak bungalows have remained an integral part of the travel experience along highways and smaller roadways in India. Built in the 1840s following a decree by Lord Auckland, the then Governor General, these rest houses, separated from one another by 12-15 miles, carried forward the long-established tradition of caravan serais and dharmshalas built by Indian rulers for pilgrims.

Dak bungalows were a convenience for British officers detailed to set up and maintain colonial outposts throughout India in the 19th century. And these were staging points for mail runners of the Imperial Mail Service, and makeshift court houses for proceedings in remote areas.

Many of these structures that have survived the vicissitudes of time are still to be found along highways, major and minor alike. Wherever possible, these were built on promontories overlooking the surrounding landscape; modest two-bedroom accommodations with terracotta-tiled roofs and planter's chairs in deep veranda affording an unrestricted view of the usually large compound dotted with trees, many fruit bearing and others for shade.

Aghori

The Aghori (Sanskrit aghora) are a small group of ascetic Shaiva monks who engage in post-mortem rituals. They often dwell in charnel grounds, smear cremation ashes on their bodies, and use bones from human corpses for crafting kapalas (skull cups which Shiva and other Hindu deities are often iconically depicted holding or using) and jewellery.

Aghoris are devotees of Shiva manifested as Bhairava, and monists who seek moksha from the cycle of reincarnation or samsāra. This freedom is a realization of the self's identity with the absolute. Because of this monistic doctrine, the Aghoris maintain that all opposites are ultimately illusory. The purpose of embracing pollution and degradation through various customs is the realization of non-duality (Advaita) through transcending social taboos, attaining what is essentially an altered state of consciousness and perceiving the illusory nature of all conventional categories.

McCluskiegunge

McCluskiegunge is a small hilly town in the state of Jharkhand, India, about 64 km northwest of the capital, Ranchi. It was founded by the Colonisation Society of India in 1933 as a homeland for Anglo-Indians. Anglo-Indians could buy Shares in this co-operative – The Colonisation Society of India – which in turn would allot them a plot of land. It became home to 400 Anglo-Indian families within ten years.

In 1932 Ernest Timothy McCluskie, a businessman from Calcutta, the founder of the town, sent circulars to nearly 200,000 Anglo-Indians in India inviting them to settle there. Of the nearly 300 original settlers, very few families remain now, as most of the Anglo-Indian community left in the 1950s and 60s. The town has lush green surroundings, dirt tracks and fresh air to breathe.

Battle of Henkar

Henkar till this day exists as a forward post of the Indian Army in Arunachal Pradesh. It witnessed heavy fighting during the 1962 Sino-Indian Conflict. Henkar Post is located about 25 km north of Manigong in present day West Siang district of Arunachal Pradesh. Major PA Rege of 11 Assam Rifles was the officer commanding the troops positioned at the post for the defence of Manigong valley.

On 24 October, 1962, a large number of Chinese troops attacked Henkar post. Major P.A. Rege and his troops, though greatly outnumbered, fought back so tenaciously that they repulsed four enemy attacks and inflicted heavy casualties on them. Ultimately after hand-to-hand fighting our troops had to withdraw. However, in the process, Major Rege and his men successfully blocked the advance of the enemy for a considerable period, thereby allowing reinforcement of the rear echelons and moving up of Artillery pieces. For his outstanding leadership, gallantry and complete disregard for his own safety, Major PA Rege was decorated with the Vir

Chakra, the India's third highest gallantry award.

There exists a small memorial next to the post commemorating the Battle and in remembrance of those who laid down their lives in the battle.

Caranzol Railway Station

The privately owned West of India Portuguese Railway (WIPR) extended 83 km from the port of Mormugão in Portuguese colony of Goa to Castle Rock in the Goa/British India frontier. At Castle Rock it merged into track built by the Southern Mahratta Railway Company (SMR) for 111 km from New Hubli located in the Dharwar District of the Bombay Presidency. Construction of the WIPGR began in December 1881. The combined WIPR-SMR project was opened throughout its full length in 1888. The line remains in use in the 21st century as part of Indian Railways.

Caranzol railway station is a small railway station on this line. This station is one of three in the Braganza Ghats and is the last station in Goa before the line passes into Karnataka. While the railway line from Mormugao to Collem was laid on a relatively easy terrain, the track from Collem to Caranzol was laid on "extremely uneven and difficult terrain" which necessitated construction of a number of tunnels and bridges. In all, there are 16 tunnels along the route up to Castle Rock.

Sir Hugh Massy Wheeler

Sir Hugh Massy Wheeler KCB (30 June 1789 – 27 June 1857) was an officer in the army of the East India Company. In 1856, he was appointed commander of the garrison at Cawnpore (now Kanpur). He is chiefly remembered for the disastrous end to a long and successful military career, when his defence of Wheeler's entrenchment and surrender to Nana Sahib during the Indian Rebellion of 1857 led to the annihilation of almost all the European, Eurasian and Christian Indian population of Cawnpore, himself and several members of his family included.

Ladle (Steel Making)

A ladle is a vessel used to transport and pour out molten metals into a furnace in certain kind of steel plants. Large steel mill ladles can hold up to 300 tonnes of material. For transportation of such large volumes of molten metal, the ladle typically runs on wheels, purpose-built ladle transfer cars or will be slung from an overhead crane and be tilted using a second overhead lifting device.